THE ODDS, SODS &
of SHORT
BOOK 1
(OsssOss1)

TREVOR WATTS

Twists and Turns

Dedicated to Chris Watts
For her editing skills, commitment, and tolerance.

Log on to https://www.sci-fi-author.com/
Facebook at Creative Imagination

First Printing: 2021
Brinsley Publishing Services

BPS

ISBN: 9798594673618

CONTENTS I

CONTENTS II

A CATEGORY FOUR NAME

The way my adoptive parents told me, long before they enrolled me at Braven Boys Elementary School, was that I was found on a church doorstep in July 2019. 'So we reckon your birth mom had some faith in religion. The church ladies promptly cleaned you up, wrapped you up and took you to the hospital—'

'Where they had a unit for castoffs like you.' My new dad always told it like it was.

'It was their obligation to register foundlings with the police and the authorities. And, of course, fill in the forms and make it official – including a name for you.'

'Rather than go down an alphabetical list,' Mum said, 'or their cats' and dogs' names, like anybody normal, the nurses apparently liked to have a laugh. They picked first names by watching the TV, and, once they sat down, the first personal name that appeared on screen was what the baby got.'

'It had to be on screen,' Dad butted back in, 'because they didn't know how to spell some of the weird monikers they have these days. Second names, or surnames, they picked by the first *place* that was spelled out.

'It happened that when they turned the TV on, it was the news – which is usually good, apparently,' New Mom told me, 'because they get lots of names and places straight away. The big thing on the news was this category 4 hurricane scooting round the Gulf and heading for the Louisiana coast a bit west of New Orleans.'

'That sounds dodgy,' I said, when they were telling me. 'So I just avoided having a family name of New Orleans or Louisiana?'

'You can thank the Good Scheduler in the Sky for not putting them names on the screen, eh?' Dad laughed about that, alright.

'What popped up on the screen was, "Hurricane latest – Barry nears land at Lafayette."'

'So that was agreed, to much merriment, I'm told.'

Thus, I am Barry Nearsland Lafayette.

Pretty smart huh? Barry Nearsland Lafayette. Name fit for an artist or a movie producer or a novelist, although I really want to follow Dad in the design and construction business; he runs the biggest building firm in town.

I am just so lucky. When I think that a week earlier, I would have been Andrea Yucatán Peninsula. One week *later*, I'd have been Chantal Horseshoe-Beach Florida. I don't think I would have survived Kindergarten at Braven Boys.

ME AND MY TUM

I suppose you've seen these sci-fi films where somebody gets a body-part transplant, and they start to take on the traits or emotions of the donor. And they never suspect anything until things get really weird.

Well, I had this transplant a few weeks ago, and I'm beginning to wonder.

For instance, I remember back to a film back in the 60's or 70's where the bloke had a penis-called-Percy transplant. He turned into a right Don Juan. Everso entertaining, it was, all driven by the randy donor's dixie. I don't think they've done a vagina transplant yet, and I don't want to be the first. But that wouldn't really be an option for me, I suppose.

Quite apart from that – I'm going red-faced just thinking about that – there's been at least one film where somebody had a new hand and it kept doing things, like strangling people or shooting them. I don't like to watch them: it makes me sort of creepy-crawly inside and I look at my own hands and wonder if it could happen to me. I even pretended to go all zombie-like and staring-eyed and put my fingers round my throat, clawing at myself. But Mary came in and she was just being stupid about it and laughing at me. So I wouldn't make her cocoa.

There was that woman who had a new heart – it was in the paper and on the telly, so I think it might have been true. And she fell in love with the widower of her donor. That was quite sweet, actually. I sometimes wonder if they're still together, and imagine their other halves making out up in heaven. And who could blame them, if they're looking down and watching?

It's not like I was ever all that interested before, but since I had my transplant, it's been on my mind a modicum. I remember another one about a man who had replacement lungs and they were huge and he became a champion runner or something like that. Plus, I was just watching a video where a woman had corneal grafts and she started seeing ghosts and apparitions. That one scared me and I didn't watch it all. Made me shiver, it did.

So now, I'm wondering if there's any real truth in the idea. I've looked on the net, and there's lots of tales about it – the usual nutters and morons who didn't read what the original question on the blog was – and some that could be genuine links between the transplanted part or organ and subsequent changes in behaviour. But there haven't been any scientific studies of a large sample of subjects. They're all anecdotal – which, by definition, is, well, anecdotal. They're merely odd stories that might, or might not, mean something. But they haven't been analysed for common factors or outcomes; no predictions or blind groups to check them against.

My transplant is a new stomach. They're not common because people can generally manage without a stomach, as long as they take all kinds of pills instead. But, with some of us awkward folk, there's a clash between pills and my metabolism, and it means I did need the transplant.

What worries me, just a tad, is who it might have come from: they haven't told me yet. From what I researched on Google, it could even be a pig's stomach. That made me wonder if I might start wanting to eat worms or grass or whatever. Or, if it was from some Jamaican guy, would I be addicted to ackee fruit and goat soup? Chinese or

4

Indian would be alright, because I like curries and rice and noodles.

German? Nothing much there, I suppose – hamburgers and pickled cabbage? American? Hot dogs plus surf'n'turf are about their limit. Or Scottish – I'd be living on haggis toasties and deep-fried Mars bars.

It was all fairly general in my thinking, conjecturing a wisp of fancies to amuse myself till Mary comes to take me home. I haven't been eating anything solid or tasty or even very recognisable. My stomach and bowels need to become accustomed to digesting the easy stuff first. No, what started to specifically bother me was a telly programme I was watching the other day. It was really good, and I was thinking, 'That one's smart... Oh, yes, *there's* a tasty one... I could fancy that one. Nice pair of legs on that pale one... Oh, yesss...'

It was a David Attenborough documentary. They were *frogs!* Oh, God! No! I've got a French guy's stomach!

RETAIL FEVER

I must go down to the shops again,
To the lonely shelves and the till.
And all I ask is a facial mask
And an anti-virus pill.

I'll calmly queue two metres apart
Around the car park – twice if I must.
I'll wipe the trolley and wash my hands
And wipe away the gathering dust.

I'll only buy one pack of each
Not stack my shelves with toilet rolls.
One tin of peas and one of beans,
And placidly meet the government's goals.

Hurriedly, I'll dash back home,
And wait until my stress abates.
Then pour a glass of new-bought wine.
'Yes, yes,' I'll gloat, and unpack the crates

Of Pinot Noir and Chardonnay,
Of Sauvignon and French Merlot
And stack them high on the garage floor.
'Oh, yes,' I'll smile, 'I cleared that shelf,
                    and the one below.'

A PURPLE NIGHTIE

'What on Earth is that going off for?' I drag out my bed and open the door – the alarm was going off. Plenty loud enough to waken the heavily sedated, if not the dead.

So I slip my night-dress on and go into corridor, wondering… *No sign of smoke*, I'm sniffing round, not a whiff or a wraith. Nor any other guests come out their rooms.

I went down. The foyer was deserted – the alarm still clanging away. 'Oi! Anybody?'

Couple of other guests came down, wondering, shrugging, 'It'll be another false alarm – one last week…'

'I'm going back to bed.' Sure enough, they looked round, mouths open, eyes shut, and staggered back up the stairs.

I went round the back of the desk, into a little office. A young feller was there, fast off. He refused to wake up – all befuddled. Wouldn't get up when I dragged his feet off the couch.

'It's always happ'ning. I'll do the reset.' But he was sinking back; he'd been on something.

'*You* might be able to sleep, but I can't, not with that rattle.' So I went to have a look round…

The ground floor seemed to be clean of any smell or smoke, so I went back to the upstairs corridor, and there it was – a smell of smoke. Coming out the ceiling vents half-way down the corridor.

'So, it's in the roof space. Urghhh, I don't like the look of that…' Several access boards had smoke puthering round the edges. 'There's some pressure building up the other side of there,' I'm telling myself, like a running commentary. 'Serious, this is…'

I ran down that corridor banging on doors and shouting, and then down the corridor in the other direction from the lifts…

I come back. There's one door open. All the rest stayed shut. 'Might be empty,' said Droopy Eyes – this guy who came out in pink pyjamas.

'Not all of'em. Can't be…'

He's getting his missus and kids together and herding them out.

'Down the stairs!' I shouted at him, 'not the lift.'

'I'm not carrying all this down three flights of effing stairs,' his missis cussed me, 'Specially not dressed like this.'

So I'm going along the corridors again, all on my own and the smoke's getting worse and nobody's coming out – Ah, one came out, and he says, 'There's definitely somebody in 109.'

So I'm giving that one some fist and bellowing, and my wrist really hurt suddenly. I imagine I broke something then. It was swollen anyway – both hands were swelling. So the man in 107 went down to have another go at the desk youth, and I went round both corridors again, slamming the doors with a door-stop, and I really gave them doors some hammer, yelling, 'Fire! Get out! You'll die! Fire!' That fetched'em out – nearly every room had somebody coming out then, moaning.

'The alarms are always going off…'

'There's always somebody in the corridor after midnight playing football or rugby – sloshed out their minds.'

'Best to ignore it usually – feller on the desk never does anything about it…'

Talk of the devil! There he was, Gormy from the foyer, looking up at the ceiling access boards – now really smoking out and smelling too – that horrible rubber and plastic-burning stink.

'Have you called the fire brigade?' Everybody was asking everybody else. I've never seen chaos and stupidity like it.

'Who's been smashing these doors?' He's more concerned with battered doors than joining my effort to wake folk up and getting people out. Then he decides he'd better check that there really is a fire before calling for help.

'It might be nothing…' and he gets a broom from the service room next to mine.

I'm saying, 'No! No! No!' But he knows best, and I'm twenty yards away at the top of the stairs telling folk they can't use the lift, 'Get down the stairs.'

He pokes up at the access board, going like, 'It's my hotel and I'll do what I like. So shurrup, you c—'

Up his broom goes. Up goes the board like it's on a spring. And down comes this massive blast of flame and smoke. Down he goes. Swamped in it. Fire all round him and he's screaming for a second, then just thrashing and I'm stood there looking and empty, like, 'This is real! Oh, Shit! It's happening.' And there's this flame comes gushing at us, all silent and like sucking and radiating scorching hot and I'm turning and shoving'em down the stairs and we're all shouting our heads off and we go stumbling and falling down and there's more people down there and the lift's stuck and they can't get it down or open it.

'Is the fire brigade coming?'

'Oh, somebody'll will have—'

'*You* ring. Now! Make sure.' I ordered somebody, but he was the sort you never tell anything to, and he was going outside and me and a woman in a purple nightie went all down the ground floor rooms, battering on the doors – and there were still people in them!

Coming out, and they're all milling round in the foyer. And me and her are trying to shove them out. 'It's not safe in here.' We're telling'em and we're shoving them and they're coming back in.

'It's raining cats and dogs out there,' and they block up the revolving door. So that's jammed and they have to use the single door at the side of it.

So everybody inside is all screaming and yelling and then there's suddenly all this fire dripping down the stairwell, like melted plastic. That got'em worried and they were desperate to get out and get wet then.

And they all had their phones out to film it... 'Have you used that effing thing to call for help?' They look at you blank, or turn away so you can't see what they're doing, or think you're going to nick their phone.

The whole place was a mass of fire by the time the Fire Service arrived, well over half an hour after I went down and talked to Drippy behind the Desk. We all got pushed back on the grass and in the car park – and some folk went driving off! 'I'm not stopping here with all this going on,' some woman's saying.

Then this red-faced geezer comes demanding round, all uniform and bossy. He was the one who'd been pushing and shoving us away an hour ago. Now he's deciding he needs to know if there's anybody still in there, and I'm saying, 'There was the desk feller but he's dead upstairs.'

But straight away, he's pushing me back like I don't know anything, and he don't want to know what I've got to say, 'We decide who's dead. You're not the coroner, are you, dear?'

And he's just ordering me back again when I'm saying, 'In the lift – five of them... and some of the upstairs rooms...'

'Stop interfering.' And he's pushing me back again, so he didn't really want to know at all, even about the family that must still be in the lift.

The woman in the purple nightie got in her car, 'I'm pissed off with this lot,' she was saying, 'I'm soddened and froze.' And off she went off.

Everybody wanted statements the next day – and the day after... and four days after that – They act like they own you – the Police and Fire Service. They each had their own 'Yes-No' questions and an attitude all of their own, as though nobody else mattered, especially me – being so little and skinny. Yet I'd been there and seen Stupid get burned up like a hog roast, and I smelled him burning, and... and... and they never asked me or said anything to me about what I saw, or what I did. 'You have to stay close. We may need to speak with you again.'

'I want to see—' But they always went away, very quickly... *Want to see my hubby and my kids. I really need to.*

It was a week before they got all the bodies out. I was interviewed again. Very formal, challenging, as if I started the damn fire because I saw where it was, and made all the noise about it.

All so detailed, wanting to know who was where and who did what and who said what, and the people trapped in the lift... The moment the roof fell in and took the whole lower floor as well the top. There wasn't a single room that wasn't completely gutted. Bodies found in seven rooms; three in one that was let to a businessman on his own.

The inquest starts tomorrow; it's been swallowed up by a public inquiry, and I'm down as a witness, along with lord-alone knows how many others – 39 rooms'-worth, minus the ones who didn't make it – plus the firemen and other emergency people. And whoever did the electrics and insulation, I expect. No staff – the only one on duty was Sleepy Joe from behind the desk, and he's dead. 'The last thing he said,' I told them at the inquest, 'was, "Shurrup, you silly cow."'

Funny, but over the past seven months I haven't shed a single tear for them, not one tear, and not for any person: not the ones who answered the door and told me to eff off; nor the ones who went back in to collect something just before it all came down; nor the family stuck in the lift after I'd bellowed at them to use the stairs. Bet she didn't look too great then.

Not the ones I could smell burning, roasting, and hear them screaming, and see two faces screaming and battering at fire-filled windows.

Not a single tear.

Not until today, when I had an epiphany as to what the authorities really thought. Somebody had collated all the witness accounts, and the insurance companies had been informed of the extent of the damage – *Total*, nothing reclaimable. But they'd gathered it all together, and this morning I received their conclusion in the post – I owe them £8,201.52 for the "wilful damage caused to 39 doors by your violent actions prior to the conflagration."

14

That really hit me – money for damaged doors – that was all they thought of the ghastly deaths of eighteen human beings.

That started me off. I haven't stopped crying since.

And, with attitudes like theirs all round me, I just can't see an end to it.

VECHI SÂNGE'S COUGHING FIT

'I suppose it's a nice and clean sort of doctor' place,
Vechi,' I said. Looking around the bright plastic seats and
ivory-coloured walls with notices telling us not to be nasty
to the doctors or staff on the desk.

'I don't need telling that,' Vechi said, when I
translated for him. 'I've never misbehaved yet.'

'I expect it's because they have bother with the
locals,' I said, looking at this couple across the other side
with their sniffles and two fat children.

'Are you sure it's best for us to see a separate doctor
each? I mean – one would learn so much, add it all
together.'

'We talked about that, Vechi,' I said. 'Better to have
two professional opinions, and then we can share their
expertise, and we can pool all four views.'

'What's that say? The notice there?'

'The one with the green feller?'

'Yes. He looks like me, dunne?' Vechi adopted his
special green-fang look at me.

'Vechi,' I said. 'Not here. Not out in public. Sniffles
and co might be watching. Put yourself away.'

'Mr Vechi Sânge!' A white-uniformed woman stood
at a door, holding it open and looking round.

'Vechi, that's you, I'll see you right here after we've
both been in.'

Off he shambled – he puts that on; he can walk as well
as I can.

'Mr Nou Sânge!' Ah, my turn.

Vechi was there when I came out, 'Oooh, am I relieved to see you, Nou.'

'Tell me all about it on the way home. Come on.' I took Big Bro's arm and led him out the double doors into the fresh air. 'Nice, this English air, isn't it? Feels fresher than the Old Country.'

'That whole time in there was confusing from the start, Nou. She thought my name was Simon Sohodol.'

'No? Our village?'

'And then, she was trying to make me feel at home, and was saying words in something foreign.'

'Yes,' I said, 'mine did that. Polish. They think we're all Polish. I put mine right, and wrote Romania down for him. He said I spoke very good English, considering I'd only been in the country two weeks. I told him we'd been here for three weeks, in this village for two.'

He said, "New Nou, eh?" and I said that was what Nou meant – New. He asked if Sânge means Blood. He's a doctor, so he uses words like that.

'So I enlightened him, that our names mean New Blood and Ancient Blood, and we're brothers, sort of; brought up in the same coffin. But I don't think he has a sense of humour. Not like ours, anyway.'

'My lady doctor kept muttering to herself while she was having a quick leaf through my notes, and saying what remarkably good English I speak. So I told her we just seem to absorb it from people we get to know, as we go along, eating and drinking.'

'Vechi! Don't keep giving me your green-eyes look. It's not funny when people might see you out here.'

He sniffed and squirled his eyes back to normal – well, not normal, exactly, but near enough.

'She was asking about our medical records; said she hadn't seen any like them outside a museum – parchment and vellum in rolls and calf-skin bindings. Mostly in some very ornate and foreign language, she said.'

'It'll be because your early notes are in *Transylvanian* stràromâna, I expect, Vechi.'

'Mmm, she kept sniffing at them.'

'That'll be the rue and sage, with oregano and a sprinkle of thyme – ward anything off with that lot.'

'Never worked on me,' Vechi said. 'She seemed to weigh mine in her hands, more than look at them, and asked if they were really written with quill pens. She hardly read anything, photocopied the top sheet and said we'd have to start all over again – all smiles. Took blood tests.'

'They should ring a few bells. As long as they don't do a DNA test, eh?'

'Oh, I meant to say, right in the middle of it all, I was hacking and chest-roughing a bit – like my usual ones for five minutes when I nearly cough my lungs up. And she asked if I have coffin fits very often. Like for three weeks or more.'

'And you said?' I had a bad feeling about this.

'I told her I'd been in a coffin since I was born, but I don't need a fitting for a new one, thank you very much. I haven't changed much since the last one.

'Course, she looked at me a bit funny, and asked, as a matter of interest, when did I last have a coffin fit?'

'And you said, Vechi?'

'The truth, just before we went to meet that woman they thought was a witch.'

'Goblin Mary, yeah. She was a toughie, wasn't she? We both had a fitting then, didn't we? Just in case.' Some of these old dates get mixed up in my head. I don't know how Vechi keeps track, with twice as long to remember. 'When was that?'

'Like I told the doc lady, "I haven't had a coffin fit since Halloween 1647."'

'And how'd she take that?'

'She smiled, real nice. I think we're going to like it here, Nou.'

BISOPROLOL

I thought at first it was just Dr James, my usual GP playing a game: however I pronounced the name of my medication, he would pronounce it differently. Just being awkward to amuse himself.

But he wasn't available when my blood pressure went right down, so one of the other docs reviewed my medication.

'I see you're on the minimum, starter dose of Bisoprolol Fumarate,' Dr Mary Fairie said, pronouncing it very emphatically, "*Bye*-so-pro-lol".

And I laughed quizzically, 'Dr James always calls it, "By-*sop*-r'lol"?'

'Hmm,' she kept her eyes locked on the computer screen. '5 milligrams per dose, once a day. We'll do the bloods again. Come back next week.'

So back I went. 'Okay, does my dosage need to change?'

She stared at the screen and tapped the keys, 'The *Bissss*-op-r'lol? Yes. We'll double it. Same dose, twice a day.'

Unwisely, I know, I remarked, 'Oh, *Bisss*-op-r'lol now, is it?' When I got over her funny look, I thought, 'Two can play that.' And I said, 'Dr James said "Bi-sop-*roh*-lol."'

'Well, I'm not Dr James.' She peered over the rim of her spectacles. 'Here's your prescription. We need to review the rest of your medication, Mr Pfizer. Good day.'

As the pharmacy was next door, I popped in to have the prescription filled. The young assistant chap glanced at it, 'Ya, sir. We've got *Byzzzz-oh*-prolol in stock, sure enough.'

Southerners – don't you just love'em, eh? So they're in on the conspiracy, are they? I could tell from the look in his eyes. He took the paper round the back to find the pharmacist.

A few moments later, a little head appeared over the screen – the pharmacist – and he shouted, 'The By-*zopp*-r'lol?'

'Ay up,' I thought, 'another one.' So I raised my hand, 'The Bissopr'-*lowl?* Yes, it's for me.'

He gave me a dubious look, nodded and passed it to a young lady helper. She came wiggling up, 'Confirm date of birth. Post code? Right. Here, your *Byzo*-pr-lol.'

There is definitely a plot against me. They're all at it. 'Ah,' I said, 'They've taken me off the *Bizz*-opp-row-*loll*, have they?'

That took the silly smirk off her face, and she went back to confer. Returning, 'Yessir. It's Bisso-*proh*-lol you're on now.' A triumphant smile she gave me, adding, 'Your other medications need to be reviewed before they can be re-issued, Mr Pfizer.' She turned on her heel and wiggled away.

'This looks more like Bys-*oh*-pr-lol,' I called after her, but she carried on without reply, and vanished round the back.

**

I know it's not me; it's definitely them. They clearly have some secret system for pronouncing it differently every time. They probably have a network of shared ideas for new ways of saying Bye-*zoh*-pr'lol.

I'm on to them now – I know what they're up to.

What I don't know is *why* they're doing it.

This just isn't doing me any good.

God help me when they review my anti-paranoia medication – Zuclopenthixol Decanoate.

YEAR 9

'My client, your honour, had had a rough day when the alleged incident took place. We wish to plead extenuating circumstances in the lead-up to the incident.

'It is our contention that my client suffered from a momentary lapse in sanity: he was not in any way responsible for his actions.

'Yes, your worship, he has possibly recovered sufficiently to tell you in his own words, though he may find it difficult: he has become extremely emotional when recounting this of late.'

'Well, let him speak, and we'll see how it goes, hmm?' His Honour peered sagely over the rims of his glasses. He thought it made him look wise.

'Yes, your lordship.'

'Are you ready then, Mr Blame?'

From the dock, Mr Blame rose, already trembling at the prospect of reliving that day. He began quietly.

'The dog, your honour, had been in the bedroom sometime in the night, and when I got out of bed, I put my foot straight in a huge dollop of crap.

'My wife thought that was hilarious, but she did her nut and blamed me when she cricked a rib with all her laughing. That was when I got the split lip.

'Then the cat had been sick on my chair.

'And the telly started smoking when I turned it on,' he wiped at his eyes with the back of a trembling hand.

'The bacon tasted like rotten fish and we'd run out of brown sauce.

'Hilda couldn't find her car keys so she grabbed mine and took my car to work.

'So I got the kids dressed and fed and saw them off to school. Then I started looking for Hilda's keys. But I couldn't find them anywhere, not even in the dog's basket, or places only the cat knows.

'So it meant running for the bus, and I'm not up to much running since the accident with the washing machine.

'I didn't have my brolly and it was pi— siling down. So I got drenched and all the kids were taking the pi— mick, when I got to school.'

'Take your time, Mr Blame… Take your time.' His Honour recognised a man with Post Traumatic Stress Disorder.

'I will, your honour. Thank you. Just after I arrived at school, Hilda texted me to say she'd found her keys in her handbag.

'And then the headmaster said I'd have to lead assembly because he hadn't prepared anything.' The unlucky Mr Blame needed a moment to calm himself, regather his temper, and bring his heart-rate down. He sipped at the glass of water.

'That was when the fire extinguisher went off in the hall and there was practically a riot in the middle of "Jerusalem", so we never got round to the weekend's football victories by the first and second teams.

'I lost my free period when I would have been preparing the handouts for the Year 10's Medieval History class. That was because it was a choice of taking Hoskins to hospital with a broken nose, or teaching Year 8 Special Needs.'

'Do you need a moment, Mr Blame?'

Wiping his brow, and a swift word with his lawyer, he decided that he could continue a little longer.

'I didn't have my car, of course, so I did maths with the Year 8 Zombies – No, I'm not, your honour – they chose their class name themselves – it's official.

'Yes, your honour – that was when I got the black eyes – an accident, they said, slamming the door in my face.

'Yes, we covered adding up to ten – pretty good for them – and they voted me best teacher of the morning – yes, your honour, their only teacher – they had the rest of the morning free.'

'Are you alright to continue, Mr Blame?' The judge was concerned about Mr Blame's increasingly fragile demeanour.

The unfortunate teacher nodded silently, and resumed, 'At lunchtime, I found I had been allocated dinner duty with the netball team, followed by the chess club, because of other staff's absences…

'My wife texted again. This time to ask if I was really fond of my Mercedes SLK. It had collected a "little scratch". Or a write-off, as the RAC was predicting.' He sobbed at the memory.

'Perhaps if I might continue from Mr Blame's sworn statement, your honour?' Receiving a nod from His Honour, the lawyer continued, 'It was in the middle of the first lesson in the afternoon, your honour, with Year 9 Extra Care Group, that the girl in question came up to Mr Blame with a blunt pencil, and she said, and I quote, "Oi, sharpen this effing pencil you effing prat."

'Mr Blame politely pointed out that he had nothing to sharpen it with. The young lady pulled out the Bowie knife – yes, Exhibit Four, your honour. And she continued with her words to my client, viz: "Well, Arse

Face, you can sharpen it with this, can't you? I ain't allowed to use a knife in class, now am I?"

'Mr Blame, your honour, at this point was rather stretched by the events of the day, and he somewhat rashly, but understandably, said, "Speak to me like that once more, you little bitch, and I'll sharpen your effing head."

'And that, your honour, is how Mr Blame came to slice off the young lady's ears in front of the Year 9 Extra Care class.'

A BOLT FROM THE BLUE

Jack found out as soon as he started at the cigarette factory: 'It's workers versus management.' Everybody on the machine floor told him so…

'Can't sneak out for a quick smoke… not allowed fags in the canteen, not any more…

'Can't even bring our own snap, in case we use the box for smuggling…

'Have to pay for our own overall cleaning…

'Dock an hour's pay if we're a minute late clocking on…

'Search us after work…

'No rest breaks – the crushing machine can't be stopped just like that…

'Don't employ enough workers to run a relief rota…

'Won't let the union in…

'It's us production workers and the maintenance engineers against the bosses. You'll see, lad.'

Jack looked up at the great rumbling, tumbling machine, with hoppers feeding into it from above. Huge drums of tobacco leaf were being emptied out in the floor overhead and thrown down into the massive steel rollers for crushing. Then into the whirling after-blades for slicing and shredding.

The machine was insatiable: the two-foot-long leaves *had* to keep coming to feed the rollers to serve the slicers; to go through the sprays for moistening and on to the conveyor for flavouring of the minced tobacco. And then to the final shredding – fairly coarse for cigars; fine threads for cigarettes; and the dust sweepings for snuff.

29

'The system's all one. It mustn't stop for man or beast,' the gaffer told him. 'So do your job right, lad. I'll be keeping my eyes on you.'

'There's a thing about this machine, Jack, lad.' Gladys told him, smart in her neat-pressed blue uniform. 'Now and again, we drop a nut or a bolt into the works...'

'It gets dragged into the hopper with the leaves, to be crushed,' Olive explained.

'And jerks the massive rollers apart,' Elsie finished.

'It's the bearing that snaps apart – it's designed to do that.'

'It takes half an hour while we're standing down for the engineers to lift the top roller, scrape all the half-mashed leaves out, find the offending object, and replace the roller bearing.'

'Naturally, we have to clear up all the leaves afterwards. Including the broken fragments of the old bearing...'

'...which are useful for tossing back in the next time we need a break.'

'The engineers keep a stock of suitable bits on the grid tray on top of the machine, in case we run out.'

'Management assume it's pieces that've come in with the leaves, from South America, or India, or Africa.'

'Eh?' Jack was getting bothered about this.

'If we didn't keep the engineers busy, the bosses'd sack half of'em. We have to look after each other, us production girls and the maintenance men.'

'So, lad, we're going to have to search you...' They were coming at him ominously.

'What? You think I'm a management spy or something?' Backing away only got him into a corner.

'No no. Just keep still, Jack lad…' Two women feeling in his trouser pockets…

'Hey, what y' doing?' He was worried now.

'Just tearing a little hole, lad.' Gladys had this triumphant smile.

'What the hell for, y' pervy gits? Get off me.'

'Need a hole there lad… bottom of y' pocket… for when you're on the top gangway…'

'When you're cleaning the overhead dust filter out, gaffer can see your hands are occupied, so it *can't* have been you, can it?'

'What can't be me?'

'The one who drops *this* into the works. So get up there pronto…'

'I'm dying for a pee…' said Gladys.

'And a coffee…' said Olive.

'And a fag…' said Elsie.

WHERE THERE'S A WILL

'It *was* tonight, wasn't it, Elly?' Slightly shocked, I stared at the door, half an inch in front of my nose.

'Yes. Definitely. I wrote it down. And the address, *here*: 6252 Chattanooga Avenue. Apartment 404.'

'So what was that about?' We both stared at the dingy mushroom door. The end one along the dim-lit passageway.

'Dunno. It *is* seven o'clock, isn't it? We've even brought a bottle *each*. Decent stuff, too.'

'Looks like we'll have to drink it ourselves.'

'That's no hardship. It is a good one.'

'Shall we pick up a TexMex on the way home? Or would a Cajun go better with the wine?'

I shrugged, 'Whichever. I never had a door slammed in my face quite like that before. Even by him. Not since we were kids, anyway. He did a lot worse then.'

'I thought it had broken your nose. You were just starting forward.'

'Yeah, it just touched.' I could feel the impact tip, as I'd already started to think of it. 'He looked furious about something. He always did, when we were kids. And took it out on me, as often as not. Little Sis me was generally the one to suffer when Big Bro threw a wobbly.'

'Yep – something rattled his cage alright. No idea what. Must have changed his mind about making up after all these years.'

He'd been smarm itself on the phone – eight years since we'd spoken. He'd moved back to Alabama and wanted to re-meet. We were all the family that was left, now dad's died.

'His sudden contact must have been pricked by your dad dying – realising there was no-one else he had left.'

'The last thing he said to me was two words, and they started and ended with F. I think it was the last thing he said to dad, as well. And probably mum, too.'

'He was always like that? Nasty to everybody?'

'Yep.'

'It makes me wonder… Does he know what the will says?'

'I don't see how. It's with dad's lawyer – tomorrow will be the first any of us knows. Unless dad wrote to him separately, I suppose. Maybe dad told him, or gave him a clue.'

'We'll find out tomorrow, then.'

Eleven sharp next day, we sat down with Mr Austin, the lawyer. Me and my hubby Eric; with Raymond and his wife Madeleine also on the visitors' side of the desk. All scowls and mutters and no mention of last night. Like it hadn't happened. So I asked him; he is, in theory at least, my brother, so I felt entitled.

'So what happened last night, Ray? The door and everything?'

He pulled a face and curled his lip, snarled very slightly, 'If you get it all, I'll damn-fluting kill you.'

'Charming. We thought you'd invited us round to have a lovely chat and talk about the great days when we were kids…'

'Yeah,' he curled a lip in our direction. 'I thought we could be friends for once. Changed my mind when I saw your ghastly twee little face, Sis. It all came back – Always making me out to be wrong. Always me the bully. That's you all over. I knew you'd be whinging about it all over again, if I let you in last night.'

He pulled another face. I remembered that uglified face from age four to nineteen.

'And when we opened the door to you last night and you were standing there with Ass-face Eric, a stupid grin and two bottles of Napa Valley You-rine, we could tell you knew – dad's left everything to you, has he? And you're just the sort of selfish bitch who won't share a red cent. Always have been.'

'Me? Not share? I seem to remember giving you every cent of my pocket money most weeks – because you just stole it. And threatened to unleash your mates on me if I didn't. You did set them on me a couple of times when I did give my cash to you as well, when you were in a bad mood. So that was your idea, was it? Butter me up, in case?'

Actually… thinking about it – I reckon it would have worked. If dad really had left it all to me, and Raymond had been nice and all make-uppy last night – yeah, I'm so soft I would have split it down the middle. For family. I'd have done it because I'm so stupid I'd believe him, yet again, about making up and being friends, and family and all that. 'Raymond. After that performance from you last night, there's no way I'd ever give you another dime.'

Mr Austin coughed that cough that lawyers and counsellors seem to perfect as an "ahem" to bring us to order, politely. He's smiling… at Raymond and Madeleine. *He's damn near in bed with them – he knows which side his bread's buttered on.*

Hell, watching them cosying-up, it's obvious: Raymond's had a tipoff. *You were going to gloat last night, weren't you? Then maybe remembered you weren't supposed to know; so you called it off in your usual*

35

manner? Yeah… he would have been smarming round, all smirks and mutters, nods and winks. Ah well, I never counted on anything – me and Eric do our own thing. We always saw dad every week, took him on holiday sometimes. But dad was a funny'un: just as likely to have left everything to Raymond, simply because he was so independent – they both were.

Yeah, ignorant, they are – Mr Austin, Raymond and Madeleine – mumbling and muttering. Sounds like Mr Austin's warning him, probably not to gloat too much. Be generous in spirit.

He's opening the folder. There's the will – already unsealed – I recognise the great big fancy lettering. So he did know… smiling kindly now, at us. Kindly? Huh – sympathetically, more like. He's talking – legalese, gibberish. All whereforeuntos and notwithstandings.

In five minutes, it's all said and done. And we're trying to figure out what it means.

So, Mr Austin explained it in English: 'Your father instructed me to liquidate all of his assets - the house, contents, cash and investments – amounting to a not inconsiderable sum…' He nodded over his glasses very sagely, 'and donate it to the Pussy Heaven Cats' Home.'

Ahh… So… I get nothing. And Raymond gets nothing. Okay, fair enough. I can sometimes see where Raymond gets his awkwardness from – but I still like dad, anyway. We were always good to each other, and good for each other. I can keep things in perspective.

'One more thing,' Mr Austin said, 'He did leave each of you one small personal gift.' He handed us a small envelope each.

Raymond tore his open in a temper, like he was going to take it out on the contents – a fancy-lettered card. 'A

Doll's House!' He yelled. '*A doll's house? What's that all about?*'

'Ah,' Mr Austin piped up, 'that will be the packing crate in the lockup garage on Fremont – for which the key is *here*. Mid Plantation Era doll's house, I believe. Made around 1780. Of some value, estimated to be well over one thousand dollars.'

Oh boy, was Raymond mad, cursing all and sundry, '*He's given it all to a darnation cat's home!?* Every dime? The stupid old redneck crudstick didn't even like cats!' He and Madeleine went storming off without so much as a "Gotta go" or "Up Yours" to any of us.

So Ray inherited a doll's house, hmm? Wonder what ours is? Let's have a look in the envelope...

'Ahh, the same sort of card...' I showed Eric.

'Well, it's not a Plantation Era doll's house...'

'It's,' I peered, 'The Pussy Heaven Cats' Home.'

37

A PICKUP IN THE BAR

Hi ho. That was the way it went. Bloody women. Disappointing, but...

One deep sigh to get over it. Right – head up – shoulders back. Big smile. What next? The hotel bar looked inviting. The barman obviously realised I'd been stood up – they don't look at customers sympathetically out of habit. 'It happens, Sir.'

'It does indeed.' I eyed him up, not wanting a conversation about being dumped and plenty more fish, etc. 'Plonk whisky and dry ginger, please.' A quiet drink, then off to my lonely garret for a few more drinks, popcorn and binge-watch The West Wing. Probably.

I sat down; a table in the middle, because all the wall and window places were full. The place was becoming crowded with couples who'd come for the sedate dancing evening in the next room – except they would pull the partitions back and it would become one big spill-over room. 'Never mind,' I sighed at my glass. 'Pity about her, though.'

'Hi, please don't think I'm too pushy, but I'd kinda like some pleasant company this evening.'

Oh, God, I thought, *I'm out the mood for company now.*

The voice continued, 'Are you free to fill in the Lonely-Me Position? Just for a time, no strings? I thought you fitted the bill for being pleasant company, you know, a bit bouncy, amused at something. It's only for the down-here part of the evening. Nothing further, up in the room. I mean, if you're on your own?'

Well, that laid it out plain enough. I turned and looked up. My sort of age, knocking thirty. Expensively dressed in a cocktail suit – is there such a thing? But, you know, like, smart.

'On my own? I *did* have a date, but it seems like my date didn't. Are you thinking of eating? Here in the hotel? Or somewhere out of here? There isn't a show, is there? Karaoke?'

Open smile. Nice face. Lived-in sort of grace. But she looked gone out at the thought of karaoke, and was obviously reconsidering her options. 'This place not posh enough for you?'

I shrugged. 'I'm eclectic; or whatever means I'm happy doing anything from a seven-course banquet up to a Chinese takeaway. Including a bar meal.'

The prospect of further social intercourse suddenly quite appealed, strictly the social kind. 'Please, be seated,' I invited, and even stood and pulled the other chair out, gentleman that I am.

She was charm itself, way out of my class, but she chattered and laughed and told tales and asked about me. She liked the Thai fishcake starter, and loved the steak with something unpronounceable. By the time we'd finished we were in full eye-contact mode and the music and light-dance evening had begun. The partitions were drawn back and the floor was ours.

Her warmth, the smile – friendly, knowing. The quizzical tilt of her head; so light on her feet. She was a goddess. So light in my arms on the dancefloor. She flowed to perfection, was warm, was everything. I was shaking. Entranced didn't come into it: I was beguiled. *Awking Fussom,* I said to myself. I had lost my breath to her. We danced. We wined and laughed. The most amazing evening.

It's too perfect. I was getting frightened-rabbit-frozen. Good things simply do not happen to me. I just knew it was all about to collapse. The pumpkin coach would arrive soon and she'd be gone and I'd still be here. I had to go before that could happen. I was stumbling, getting in a panic. 'I gotta go.'

'What is it?' She was stopping me leaving. 'Danny, it's a dance. It's just an evening. That's all we said.'

'I'm sorry, Myla. I'm too far gone for you – I'm in love at first dance. I can't face being dumped on the stroke of midnight.'

Oh, Danny, I like you. But I... don't feel the same about you. I love your twinkle; the little jokes. I like you a lot. Don't go, please. Let's give it a chance. Maybe... Later, we could—'

She was trying to help.

But nothing could. What I was feeling for her was too pathetically intense and getting worse. *Oh, God. I've fouled it up. Precipitated it.*

Her eyes glistened. *She's acting?*

Damn. I felt my tears welling up. Looking blurredly round at the other dancers, some laughing, some smiling, all stepping lightly, twirling. A big screen with some cartoon characters dancing and swaying. The slowly spinning mirror globes sending tiny beams around the walls. The speaker lights flashing and strobing. All sound and colours and movement and lights. There were lights outside, too, glaring like searchlights, growing, moving. A few people near the windows were getting up.

The lights bounced up.

Crashhhhh!!! The most almighty blast. The windows exploded inwards.

41

A scream. Cut off. A huge vehicle front was airborne, above head-height. Dropping. Engine roaring, lights blasting, horn bellowing.

It was flying straight at us. Glass exploded everywhere, all over everyone like an instant crystal shower. I don't recall thinking. I shoved her down. Same time, trying to ward it off with one hand.

Ward it off? It was two tons of sodding great Toyota Pickup and I went flying back with it on top of me. I was bouncing and rolling underneath it, wheels and axle and differential churning whirling round in a blender of bits of tables and chairs and people. Roaring off me. I was churned over in a smashed-up heap. Totally shocked. Myla? *Need to sit up.* Can't. Taste and smell of blood. Something wrong. Screaming everywhere. The massive thing was rammed into the bar. Smoking. Roaring. Lights flashing all over. Invincible, it said on the back of it. Needing to see Myla. *Shit – if she's been hit?*

Grunting and gasping like a stranded pig, trying to twist over. The Toyota still revving and clonking and jerking. It lurched back from the bar, a load of glass and polished wood crashing down as it came crushing and crashing back over the tables and people. I tried to get aside. Too slow and it flattened me again. Nightmare of seeing the underneath so close and loud and dark; and the wheels missed my leg by about an inch. I saw a head crushed – burst open – God!! Short blonde hair. Blood spattering everywhere. All over my face. Head bits.

The huge thing was stuck – its backend had hit one of the pillars between the huge windows.

I was stuck, too. Couldn't move my legs. *Have I still got legs?* Wanting to reach and feel… can't tell. Vaguely aware of people around me, people fallen. Shouts and screams. Some going for the driver. Fighting and shrieking.

Stink of blood and smoke. Engine still roaring. Trying to move again. Screaming. The driver dragged out. The engine faded and cut. Clouds of smoke from somewhere underneath. Weird, lurid with strobe lights still piercing through.

All sobbing… crying loud then, screaming names, crawling. Someone pulled at me. She was looking for someone else. I touched at myself. Thank God – can move a bit. God, so shaky. Perhaps not try to get up again. Not yet.

Lights off. Dark then, smoke thick-tasting. Distant lights now, flashing.

'Danny. You alright? I thought… when it reversed over you…' Myla was there. Panicking, wild-eyed, clutching at me; pawing at my clothes like she was checking I was still in them.

'Yes, I'm okay. Fine.' I had no idea whether I was okay or not. I just said it. 'Need to wait a minute, make sure. You? You alright?'

She was nodding ten to the dozen, holding me tight, in all the glass and broken chairs and people. Clutching at me, holding my head like it was going to fall off. Looking around at the wreckage. Touching down me, making sure I was all there, I thought.

This face above me, dark-shrouded, worried. She pressed me down when I tried to move, 'Don't move. You're still in one piece.' Face suddenly smiled, fingers down my cheek, 'That's two pickups there's been in here tonight.'

THE WOLF WHISTLE

One wolf whistle in that situation is one too many.

I mean, I'm the office stunner. The posh one. The aloof one. I'm *Unapproachable.* I am far above and beyond common wolf whistles.

Coming to an abrupt halt, I turned to face the miscreant and treated him to my most icy glare.

I was looking down on a squirt of a creature – dark suit, flat hair, scrubbed grinning face.

From my six-feet-four, in six-inch heels, I towered over the happy little grinner who evidently thought he'd scored some sort of triumph to stop me in my tracks and pay attention to him.

He was mistaken. It was the first nail in his coffin.

I glared. Waited for an apology.

I didn't receive one. 'Well, smart bird like you,' he chanced instead. 'What do you expect? Swanning through here like Lady Docker?'

I refuse to respond to such comments: I *am* Lady Docker here. I have perfected this lip-curl – not too much, but clear enough – and I turned it on.

Ant-like happy-chappy didn't even notice. 'Well? What do you say? You and me, eh? How about it?'

'How about what?' I was aware of the whole office paused in its machine-like bustle; every staff member's life on hold: this would be their talking point for days between the water dispenser and the copier.

'You know. Me and you… Tonight?'

Inside, I hovered between affronted and entertained. I stiffened up and eye-narrowed. 'And what did you have in mind, Little One?'

'Ah, since you're asking,' he raised his voice, so others could hear his jovial banter more clearly. 'What I thought was a couple of drinks, meal and a bottle at Jebero's, then back to my place, hmm?' That appallingly cocky little toad-faced twat.

'Oh? And then what? Scrabble?'

'Well, you know…'

'No, I don't know.' I gave him my finest Estée Lauder All Day Frosted Strawberry Lipstick smile.

'We could be making out from nine till five; me and you.' Big grin all round. Faces neutral to aghast among the office populace.

'Making out?' There's nothing like pretending to be dim when you have a smirky little idiot like this, 'I don't know what you mean.' The office was virtually silent by then; a telex chattering somewhere… an answer machine bleating.

'Yeah, you do. You know…' His edge was blunting a mite then. 'You know…?'

'Ohhh, you mean you want to…?' My best ice-maiden stare bored down into his blankly sparkling little eyes.

'Yeah… fuck you. How's about it, eh?'

I leaned down to whisper in his ear, 'And fuck you, too, my little turd.' I could almost hear it echoing through the empty vault therein.

As I stood back to my full height, he looked suitably taken aback, and I took my turn to raise my voice for the benefit of the host of listeners. 'I can only assume which planet you obtained your Green Card from, but you can collect it from the front desk of the Employment Office on your way out, and take it back to Your Anus. Hmm?'

The look of shock was gorgeous. There was my reputation – reinforced and soaring. I've no idea who he was – some new creep in Finances who fancied himself.

46

I managed to keep a straight face all the way through the main office. No-one in there had much idea who I was – they assumed I was some senior management officer promoted too soon through a bed somewhere? Boss's daughter sinecured into a top job? They had no real knowledge – only that I sailed through here twice a day, all glammed-up six-feet-four-in-six-inch-heels of me. The epitome of glamour.

That should be entertaining, when Happy-Chappy goes to the Employment Office and explains why he'd been fired. The staff on the front desk will look baffled, until one'll pretend to catch on, 'Oh, Isobel Lorraine? You crossed *her*, huh?' They'll tut a few times; shake their heads; look at each other and smile, and say something like, 'Don't take it too seriously this time; she doesn't usually mean it for a first offence. Just behave in future, hmm?'

There. Reaching the far-end door, I felt like brushing my hands together in a symbolic "job done" gesture.

It's only in the Employment Office, where my pop's the manager, that they actually know me. Because I work in the back office there.

I'm actually George MacGregor, the transgender guy. My word, would Happy Chappy have been surprised if he'd got me into bed.

BAKSHEESH BILL

He's still in there, of course, the pilot. He's moving a little – a hand... eyes... glazed and bloodied.

The cockpit canopy is split and cracked – the airframe had twisted on impact. One wing had almost snapped off. The plane had come in flat, the undercarriage crushed underneath, no sign of it. Sprayed with machine gun holes, much of the fuselage had taken hits. They look more like Spitfire calibre than Hurricane, but the Spits aren't due to be moved in and operational for another week – and that is top secret information. Only the most senior ground crew know, so we can do the preparation for their arrival – the jigs and spares, degreasing... training on them, poring over blueprints and pages of instructions... unpacking spares for repairs, double air filters for the desert dust.

But this one's German. A Messerschmitt 109. *The enemy.* Such finds were well worth checking for any new developments, fire power, engine improvements, ammo capacity. Peering inside the broken wing... yes... I can dismantle the guns. Start on the engine, too, to analyse the power output. The boffins would check that, back at HQ.

But the pilot... He's still alive. What am I going to do about him?

Bill Harwood was a great bloke; life and soul of the party and the cycling club. Always dependable, always there for a laugh. Do a favour for anybody. Stone cold sober every minute: he never felt the need for drink to loosen him up or brighten his day. Nor did he swear – his father had been too much of a drunken low-life to get into booze and profanities. His single surrender to evil was smoking his pipe.

Stocky and strong, Bill was honest as day. A keen cyclist, liked and relied on by everyone in the Clarion... the weekend camping meets... the soccer team... and presently in the Egyptian desert and places around... like Libya and Tunisia... Morocco and Algeria. Crew chief now. Leading Aircraftman.

Baksheesh Bill, he was known as: he always tossed a coin, a sweet, or a tin of bully to the kids round the camp. The *al'atfal* waifs were always there, begging, stealing, or wanting work jobs, '*Baksheesh, baksheesh, effendi. Raja.'.'* But what they stole wasn't as much use to the British Army as it was to the kids and their families. Besides, they paid their way – four times this year they'd pinpointed the site of downed aircraft – three of ours; one of Jerry's.

Bill invariably had a pocketful of sweeteners for the camp kids. They steal from him; and they did tell him about a German spy in town, and the crashed aircraft.

It was only the once that he'd dreamed of being a pilot – who hadn't? Nobody who'd read Biggles, that was for sure. That one time of dreaming was when he flew downhill on pedals and wheels, the wind in his hair, arms out wide like wings. Girl by his side, not a care in the world. The bend at the bottom of the hill was sharper than he'd thought, so the crash was inevitable, really. The girl gave him up, *and I'm giving up thoughts of flying, if that's what crashing a bike is like.*

Thus he became a mechanic, a top notch one, too. He knew tools and torques and spanners and gauges. So he became an aircraftman, first class. And he worked on the planes, kept them flying, fixed them up, suggested improvements, advised the pilots, and organised the airfield's maintenance schedules, as well as all the spares harvesting and crash rebuilding.

This morning, like I often did, I drove the half-track into the desert after downed planes. At the moment, I'm eight hours out from base camp at this Messerschmitt. An hour ago, I dropped Dusty and Corporal Rice off at the Tankbuster Hurricane we'd part-stripped last week. They can be getting on with it, and loading the trailer. It's got the fuel lines, pumps and engine parts we need to fit into a shot-up plane back at the airfield. We need that one in the air within two days. The German tanks at Kidney Ridge would benefit from the attention only the Tankbuster can provide.

Shot down yesterday, this one had been reported simply as "downed aircraft", no identification. Too little time for the spotter pilot to get close: he reported a pair of JG27s circling overhead, and had scooted smartish. Now, at ground level, with my camouflage net over the transport, I'm taking this gently. Light my pipe. The tobacco's a bit dry, so I usually soak it in rum or the local tent-brewed spirit. There's no footprints around the plane, no shelter rigged up, or words scraped out, or clothing laid out. It had come in at a fairly shallow angle, and hadn't caught fire. The canopy was still in place. So I'm expecting the pilot to be in there. Dead or alive was even Stevens. No rush, enjoy the peace and the pipe for five minutes…

Not like *my* pilot – Flight Officer Dazz Jennings. Shot down last week. Killed. Burned to death on the way down. They thought the canopy had jammed. Ah, poor Dazz, he's an amazing pilot. *Was*. Poor Dazz. I can't

51

imagine how it was. Yes I can. I've seen the awful mess they're in when they've gone down burning. Oh, gee, Dazz… the terror; the pain; the awful raging thoughts of what he'd be missing – so looking forward to life after the war. Terrible, it had been last Thursday. Friends from birth, almost. Born a month apart and on the same street down Senty, in Nottingham. The same schools, friends, cycling club, girls…

Gone now. Murdered by devils like the Nazi pig who's in here…

I'll have to jemmy the canopy open. It's a right struggle – it's jammed. Ah, *there*. Done it. Oh, Shuff – gashed my finger. Yes, he's alive. Stuck; legs probably trapped. The joystick assembly is notorious for forcing back when the undercarriage was still raised. And this one took a hard landing badly, the one-oh-nine. Red-painted nose and wing-tips, this one's got. Lord, my head's cooking in this heat.

Handsome, fair hair, blue eyes. Is this the one who killed Dazz? Or do they all look the same? Like *him*, the one who'd been on the films, their Ace, claiming ninety-odd kills – like they were at a fairground. Well, they aren't. It's my friends, officers, they're killing. We're the God-side, hand in hand with right and truth. Not like this pack of Nazis. That Jerry on the films, laughing, gloating. Great grins as they were interviewed, revelling in the death they brought, waving to the cameras and the girls. Lord, what arrogant creatures they are, these Nazis. Their sheer confidence and bragging is an affront to civilisation, to all decent people.

Staring at his full-lipped, conceited face, this creature here has no right to live. He can be *my* kill. He can die the same way Dazz went. Burned alive in this Nazi coffin. Exactly what he deserves.

Yes, I will. Looking into his eyes, I see no humanity. It'll be so easy. Much easier than writing to Dazz's girl had been, Gloria. I can write to this one's girlfriend easily. We send such letters through the Red Cross to the enemy's troops and fliers. Whoever his girl is – some arrogant sneering blonde hate-bitch.

So, so tempting, how my hand's itching to slop some cleaning alcohol in there, tap my pipe out on him. Or there's enough smell of fuel already. He'll go up like an oven. So tempting…

No… no. I can't do that. He's a human being, even if he doesn't act like one. I'd never be able to look Gloria in the eye, knowing I'd done that to someone, the same as her Dazz had died.

I'll get him out, and be content with having been so close to a live one to hate in person.

Climbing a bit higher to see inside the cockpit. Yes… his legs are stuck. But the side'll open up. I'll have to be very careful, no sparks. Lord, but it reeks in here. 'Okay, Jerry, let's be having you out of here, eh?' I smiled at him, more for my own benefit than his. Yesss, peering underneath, I should be able to get a jack under the joystick assembly.

'Okay, Fritz? Let's get a rope round you, and hoist you out. Ten minutes? Zehn minute, okay? And I'll get the side here cut open first. Ten minutes, we'll have you free. It'll mean taking you straight back to the airfield for medical attention.' It was like having a two-way conversation of talking to him and myself. 'I'll have to divert to let Dusty and Corporal Rice know. I can come back for them tomorrow. Long drive, finish in the dark, though. Risky, but, looking at you… maybe you'd not survive a night out here, even if I got you as far as the Hurricane. And back to base tomorrow.' I think I kept up the running commentary the whole time I was cutting and prising the side open. 'Taking a bit more than zehn minute, eh, Fritz?'

He's not making much of a conversationalist – a few words in German. I get some German, like he said, 'Fettig swine.' Which didn't take much understanding.

'Right,' I said. 'Trying to endear yourself to me, are you? I'll get you all the way back to base tonight, so the doc can fix your legs. So try being a bit more pleasant or I'll get him to fix'em on backwards. So watch yourself.' I gave him my big grin – as always at my own jokes.

'Ick turt oik aller.' Something like that. It didn't sound too positive. No sense of humour, huh?

'Hold still, will you? Er… Nicht bewegen.' I heard an army nurse say that to some squirming private in the burns ward one time. He didn't pay much attention, either. Mind you, the state he was in, no wonder. Sight worse than this one.

He keeps shuffling and trying to ease his legs out sideways now I've managed to ease the joystick off them. So, a rope under his armpits, lift him a bit. Recheck… Yes, coming nicely. 'Zwei minuten. Just lift you up a bit more. Yesss, nearly there. Soon. Be okay, Fritz. In Ordnung. Allers in ordnung.' The docs often reassure them with that. We say it when we've fixed a plane, too. 'Allers in ordnung.'

My head stuck down by his knee, his boot's caught on something. Something projecting down there has spiked itself through the lacing, I'm thinking. It'll need cutting through, just take a moment. Quick smile to reassure him, looking up, straight into the end of his pistol. Evil hole of it six inch from my eyes. A blurred, hate-filled face beyond it.

Jeee!!! I'm twisting, frantic to get out the way. Stuck half under him. CrashBlastDamn. Everything exploded. Flash from hell or heaven. Enormous bang. I'm dead. Stupid thing to do, rescuing a Nazi. Another huge explosion, rocking me, blasting shock going through me. I'm falling away, thudding into my head... shoulder. Flat on the coarse sand. He's leaning half out the cockpit. Still the boot trapping him; another blazing shot at me. Missed! But there's flame round his feet now – must have been the leaking fuel, set off by the first blast of his gun down there. He's not noticing his boots on fire. Another blast. Hit my shoulder again. I'm rolling away—

He's noticing now, glaring at the fire as if it shouldn't dare to be there; tugging, jerking, dropping the gun inside as he's reaching down the side of the trapped boot, flames round his face now as he bends, his jacket smoking. Trying to sit back, lift away, the flames higher, more intense.

I can't sit up. Watching from crawling flat on my back. So fascinating, awful – seeing a man blacken and char and scream and wave his shrivelling hands around... beating at himself as he jerks and stares from eyes that have no lids now... hair ablaze... his face vanishing in the melt flesh. The fire so bright.

I cannot imagine any more dreadful death. I'd have shot him if he'd dropped the gun outside onto the sand; save him that much pain.

The whole one-oh-nine is being consumed now. Such heat! Scrabbling away. Must get away from it. The ammo was suddenly going off. Sharp blasts of high-calibre bullets firing off all round me. Crawling away, looking for shelter behind anything.

It finished in the fullness of time, the smoke dying, the flames crescendo-ing and beginning to die.

My problems now are many-fold – getting to the half-track, then into it. Patching myself up… stop the bleeding. Trying to drive back to Dusty and the Corporal. Can't see out one eye. I think his first bullet hit me there somewhere.

Pity about the Messerschmitt – the guns looked like a new type – heavier, with larger ammo racks. Maybe the one in the left wing is intact; the ammo didn't explode in the fire. Would be good to get at them.

And this Jerry who killed himself – what a curse that was – I never saved anyone's life before.

I'd have been proud to do that.

BUSKING

This is the day. *The* day. It's been the big looming thing for weeks for we lowly street performers on the ground. It's been years for the officials and builders, of course, but it sure seems like years for we work-a-day buskers. They keep coming back to us with the latest rules and do's and don'ts.

There's this VIP bod coming round this afternoon to do the official opening of the whole place – the mall and hall and conference centre and stadium and everything. and they finally revealed who it is – and I mean, she is *the* one, the Queen of Everything, Star of the UltimaNet. Anything to do with Celebrity, Fame and Fortune – and she's at the pinnacle.

'So for God's sake try to be clean – put on a bit of a show.' Mr Milldean's final words of encouragement or command amply showed what a frazzled wreck he was these days.

I'd been allocated my usual spot, where I played every Thursday, Friday and Saturday, near the water fountain statue. I should think so, too – I'm council-licensed to do my busking there. In that exact spot, all legit. It's my favourite spot, because there's a bench where I can put my instrument case and clothes and collection cap, and I get the customers from Starbucks and Costa, as well as Macky Dee's

I sing and play guitar, sometimes a saxophone for a change. We performers are stationed about fifty yards apart along the main concourse in the mall. The singers and instrumentalists are placed well apart, in alternate spots with the jugglers and sick triclists and things like that. It's so we're far apart enough to make sure our music doesn't interfere with each other.

We're all totally worked up about it – I mean, playing in front of *her* – like my absolute idol.

Ahh – there – a few dignitaries-types I can see a hundred yards off. A tight-knotted bunch, the police leading the way. Everyone fussing and hovering round together, pausing a moment to watch Harry the Mime… and moving onward… another halt to watch Mary Mary who does the kids' makeup.

And *she* was there. I caught a glimpse among them. I mean – *her* – God in Gossamer. *I'm going to see her come walking past – so close, like twenty feet away. She might even glance my way – eye contact even!*

Oh, Sugar sugar sugar, she's coming towards me, 'Whatever happens,' they told us. 'You keep playing.'

'What if she speaks to us?' The mime guy asked – *as if.* I mean, *the mime guy,* of all people.

'She's not going to. She doesn't do talking with the likes of you lot.'

Charming.

'If she asks you anything directly, you can answer.' The police super was more reasonable in his expectations.

'Just remember; you keep playing, acting, painting, whatever.' Mr Milldean wasn't always snappy like that; it's just today.

She's coming closer… That face! Everybody in the world knows that face. That sophistication, beauty, the power and talent and life in that woman. Eyes that stared out the telly, out the magazines, the internet sites. She is *it.* Walking down the concourse in my direction, all this entourage keeping a respectful distance, except some gold-chained lord or something who's smarming round her.

I'm letting it rip. Sheez! – the performance I put on. This is *the* best I ever done. I'm hitting every high note, every over-complex chord and finger-twang; the lyrics, I put every ounce of expression into them. I really ought to be recording myself. I'm out of this world – three moons round my own planet.

She's stopped, not two metres away. She's watching me. Listening. The whole song. I'm only sort of half-seeing her. I'm like on Cloud ninety-nine. *She's* listening to *me*. Like – I got Mrs God's attention! I'm concentrating too much to register her. Getting the impression of a smile. And a tiara, probably a fascinator thing and a big royal smile. And I'm absolutely surpassing myself.

I'm finished and I'm sagging. Drained…

She's coming up to me, real close.

'That was busking awesome,' she says. Eyes like sharpened-up sapphires. Pauses at my cap. And she's gone.

I'm still shaking. She was so close. For minutes! Spoke to me!

They've all gone. I'm a drained bag of nerves. We're breathing again, getting ourselves back together for the rest of the afternoon. It must be ten minutes before I see the gold-embossed card in my cap.

'Call me,' she's written.

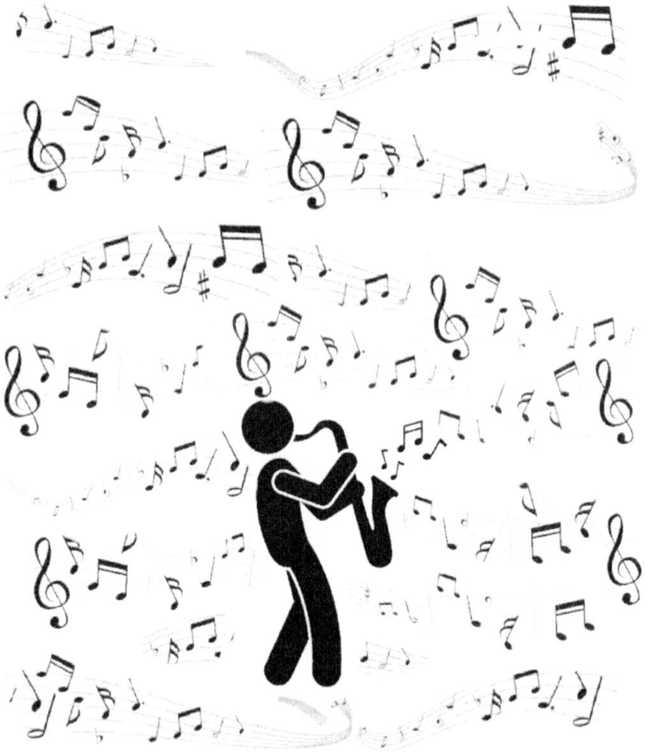

CATERING

Come on, accept it. She's ditched me.

With any kind of realism, you have to accept it when you get home and the flat is nearly empty. How I can have been so blind, I don't know. There must have been signs.

I could try to trace her, find her, go and beg... ask why... plead.

No, I couldn't. Too much pride to beg for anything. If she's chosen to leave me, that's it. She must have reasons.

Devastated hardly begins to describe how I felt. I'd thought we were made for each other. Just great together – done the flat up; planning to have a family soon. We liked so many things the same – nights out, sex, meals, films, humour... I guess something was grating with her.

It's all done and finished now. A bare flat. Even the bed and spare blankets. 'That's a mite mean,' I told the bare bulb hanging from the ceiling. 'Maybe she didn't want to give up her career; or have children? Met somebody else? Fancied a move to Tenerife?' She had mentioned several of those options, actually.

It's the sort of emptiness that eating can't fill. It's your chest and your head and your legs and bladder that are just as drained.

'I must accept that it's happened. That's first. Then accept that it's my own fault. It's of my own doing. Maybe I won't be able to pinpoint exactly what. But if I hadn't been me, it wouldn't have happened, would it?' I read that in a self-help book once. It was after that big mashup and I was looking to kill myself – you find yourself at the bottom of a pit and whichever way you try to climb out, the slopes just keep collapsing and re-burying you, and the pit gets deeper and you never see out of it. Just the slipping, sliding, gravelly slopes in every direction.

"Take responsibility for everything that happens to you," the book said. "Then you have no-one to blame and get bitter about. Only then you can start to identify the fault, and correct it; make amends, change direction – whatever it takes. Accept that you brought it on yourself."

It doesn't stop you finding a dim-lit corner down the pub to do that accepting in – it's warmer than a flat without a heater or a bed. Plus, there's plenty to drink; and there's something comfy to sit on; and nobody knows you or has any interest in you.

It does work. Beer and whiskey, that is. Blaming yourself works, too. It doesn't stop you being emptily sad and feeling a few tears drip away; and wiping them off quickly when the girl with a low top and a pinny comes up to see if you're ready to order a meal. I wasn't, but you have to buy something. So I kept my head down and pointed at the tatty menu...

'The liver and onions?' She looked dubious at my choice.

'Yes. I know,' I said, 'Spartan upbringing and all that, but I like it and you don't often see it on the menu. It's tasty. And it's cheap.'

She brought it ages later, 'Sorry it's been so long. Short-staffed.' Bent to pick something up off the floor, flouting a very fine frontage view. Bit of a blushing smile when she saw me looking. I couldn't help it. She put whatever she'd reached for on the table next to my plate. Had to smile – it was my cap, the beret with the tank corps badge. 'Yours?'

I nodded and stuffed it in my jacket pocket. My eyes brimmed up. I kept my head down and waited till she'd gone.

The meal was a touch disappointing – the liver a fraction hard, and the onions undercooked. The mash must have been okay, I suppose, because I didn't really notice it. More gravy would have helped, but my mind was on other things.

'Sweet?' She was back. Coquettish smile.

'Couple more pints?'

'You have to go to the bar for drinks. I can't bring them to the table.'

There was a queue. It took ages.

Four girls were parked round my table by the time I turned to go back. Hi ho. I'm not one for starting a negative discussion with four attractive-ish ladies who've done nothing wrong, basically. They didn't know... I looked round. Someone just leaving from two tables along, so I leapt in there before two couples who were trying to push past me. They gave me an irate mouthful as I sat down. 'It's a table for four... not just you.' They stood there, furious.

'You're worked up about a table in a pub? Tiny minds you've got.' I kept a good grip on my drinks and looked at them – the couples, and the drinks. Then I focused on my liquid sweet, and let the Nasty Four stand there and get on with their swearing.

They were gaining attention from round the bar, of one sort or another, when, 'Come on, Padsy... Derek. Don't want any trouble.' It was my Fine View Lass come to my rescue. Or their rescue, as she saw it. 'He's in the Army – A Tankie. Back from Afghanistan – he's lost mates there. He'll blow any minute.'

They departed towards the bar, awaiting another opportunity to be seated.

Fine View Lassie, smiled, 'It's my fifteener,' she said, as she parked herself with me. 'Mind if I join you? They still call it a fag break.' And slipped a double whiskey across the table towards me.

'Anybody can sit with me for that.' I think I managed a sour smile.

'Have you been back long? Bad was it? Which Regiment? Where were you stationed? My dad was in the Armoured Infantry Brigade. You got somebody to look after you?'

'I did have this morning. Not tonight.' It seemed a shame to ruin her maiden-to-the-rescue act. But I wasn't in the mood for stringing her along for entertainment, so I told her. 'All I've lost is my girlfriend. Today. After nearly three years, she's cleared off and left me. I'm working on where I went wrong. This's *her* cap – *she* was in the Tanks, not me.' I even managed a chuck – that's not as much as a chuckle.

'I got back a fortnight ago... left the army for good. And yes, it was bad – I was in the Catering Corps, and everybody moans at us.'

Right. That cooked it. Her smile faded. Miss Fine View could hardly leave quick enough now she knew I wasn't the tank hero she'd imagined. That was okay – it was a good malt she'd left. I watched her leave. She sagged a little. *Deal with it,* I thought, and wondered if Beryl had sagged a little when she'd slammed the door behind her. Probably not: Beryl never sagged at anything. Fine girl. She needed to be, gunner in a Challenger 2.

The bargirl's dad was Armoured Infantry, hmm? AI. Alien Intelligence, we called'em. Pack of thick sods.

64

I would have left, but I was comfy, and there was a really interesting stain on the floor, and the wet glass rings on the table looked like an Audi badge, or maybe the Olympics. And I was fairly sure I'd fall if I tried to stand. Funny how you think you're sober and cold-clear thinking, but hardly dare stand up, much less wend your way to the toilet.

So I sat on my own a bit longer and kept telling myself, 'Be alright tomorrow. My own fault. Mustn't do it again, whatever.'

Of course, the necessity of leaving creeps up on you as the pub vents its population into the night, and they start clearing round you, and telling you to drink up. 'You have to go…' pointing to the door. He was polite, anyway, the barman… landlord… manager… whatever. 'Catering?' he said as I very steadily rose. 'You know Sergeant Hobbs?'

'Doesn't ring a bell. There was a Sergeant Mobbs I knew. Catering's all part of Logistics Corp now, and they're mostly Reservists.'

'You'll never get home,' he told me when he thought I'd stumbled trying to turn round to see where the toilets were. 'Here, kip down in the back. Deece says y' girl kicked you out?'

'Kicked herself out, more like. Took the bed and the telly with her.'

It was a scrubby little room with a tatty settee and a couple of unstuffed chairs. 'Staff room,' he said. 'They sometimes sleep'n'slop over if we have a late sesh.'

Fine View Deece was back around ten in the morning. She even knocked. But I was up anyway. Made a coffee – had to clean a load of cups first. Place was a pit-mess. And I swept the litter out, scrubbed the sink, emptied the bins, wiped the table down. And decided I was being a total compulsive nerk and stopped. *No wonder Beryl left me.*

I did her a coffee, too, Candice. And she posed on one of the upright chairs. Nice smile – not aimed at me, though. *More like condescending,* I thought. *Catering's too mundane for you, huh?*

'Catering?' she said. 'Really? *Catering?'*

'I didn't get on with tanks. Unless they were full of porridge.' The silence was awkward. Time I'd gone. 'I'll be off. Thanks for the night's board, and the whiskey.' I rinsed my cup. And hers. 'Force of habit. Sorry.'

'No wonder she kicked you out. You're obsessive.'

'Yeah, right, and you're a psycho-doc, huh?'

'Barmaid, which is the same thing. And chef – I'm in the kitchen Monday to Thursday, five till nine.'

'Psychoanalyse the Brussels, do you?'

'I don't try to understand them; I beat the eggs and—'

'Whip the cream, yes, I know. Batter the fish? Er, there's a few things I need to get to the shops for...'

Whimsical little smile, 'Bed'n'telly?'

'And the rest. See you.'

She came tripping and trapping after me, 'Catering?'

'For chuff's sake, shut up about catering.'

'No, no. I hate cooking. We've been advertising for a chef for weeks. If you're free? Monday to Thursday? And, er, Fridays and Sat'd'ys if you could manage? Dad does it now.'

'Who did the liver and onions last night?'

'Me.'

'Oh.' I thought about it. 'I could start tonight.'

CELLO

Now, I'm a modern girl, and I don't go for stereotypes, but, we were chatting on the way in one morning, 'You act like a cartoon character.'

'Yays,' he agreed. He was a little roly-poly man with round bottle-base glasses and a wonderful sing-song accent. 'I breelliant,' he often said when he'd finalised a deal. 'I do it aall. I know thee maarkets and I do them oh-ver... That right? Do them oh-ver?' And he'd geeve mee a beeg smile. I mean "give me a big smile". And he'd beam at me, all shiny, sweaty face and bulgy eyes. 'I think I put eet on juss right, eh?'

'Er, I'm not sure,' I told him.

Gay? He was the most over-the-top camp feller I ever met, like three vaudeville acts rolled into one. 'I dunno,' I was laughing with him at the water filter. 'You're just so entertaining; you sure amuse me.' On the quiet he'd chat to me almost like he fancied me and there was nothing overtly gay there at all. But if anyone else was in earshot, he put the madly-abandoned-gay voice on, and the Oh-so-Voice and gestures. He could pose his hips – they were under the fat somewhere – and gesture like the best of the camp comedians. He'd go waddling and rolling round the whole floor – it was all one open office area with desks and booths and terminals; some private and screened, most open.

I was fairly convinced he was from somewhere Mediterranean – Spain, maybe, it was that sort of voice, but he said, 'Call-a me Chaylo.' He meant Cello –

67

because he was shaped like one, and it was his private joke. In any case, Cello's Italian, isn't it?

'You'd probably struggle to get in a cello case – or even a double bass one,' I joked with him one lunch.

It was true enough, what he said about being brilliant: I watched him, worked next to him. He *was* brilliant – a magician on the financial side, making deals I'd never have thought of. He could set them up overnight – he never slept. He knew his way through all the details and pitfalls. He was better and faster than anyone else in the firm; more thorough. I learned so much from him. Under his very informal tuition, after the first few months, I was second-best there, by a long way.

It wasn't exactly tuition – I watched what he was doing, followed him round and took notes so I could remember some of his tricks and wheezes. It's not like I finished all my degrees and articles and things like the other guys have. I was half-way through, supposedly training, but no-one had any system for doing that, so it was basically just what I picked up. 'You're getting experience of office work,' one of the knobheads told me. They all used to laugh at the idea of organising training, actually showing me anything or explaining.

Cello did, sometimes, I suppose, 'And you do-a thees like thees,' he'd rap the keys and fiddle at the screen, 'See? All ee money come thees way now…' But he wouldn't let me try it myself, and my computer outlet didn't have access to the deep internal systems that his did – with a hundred passwords and codes to protect every level.

He impressed the hell out of me – talk about admire. He was my hero, my semi-unwitting mentor. He never purposefully attempted to show me anything on a planned or organised basis; but he'd explain if I asked something specific among all the computers and wall screens and printouts and texts. But go out of his way to tell me what he was up to, and what each one meant? I don't think it ever occurred to him.

The other staff – "The Team" as they called themselves – treated him like something the cat did in the litter tray, but he just wobbled and reeled round and chuckled and outdid them all on every performance rating.

I'd often happen to have a cuppa at the same time as him – usually because I fetched two and happened to pass his station, and he'd laugh about something or nothing – he had a great sense of humour, always ready for a laugh as he waddled down the corridors of financial power. For every occasion, he had some sort of quip, half of them in Lebanese or Chinese or Something else-ese.

The others on the floor used to steal his ideas, mock him for his walk and his gestures. Or they'd ring him up from the other side of the room and take the mick out of his singy-songy accent; or try to order him round. They grabbed the credit for some of his deals; and some of the bonuses, too. Laugh about him behind his back. Give him the crappy contracts, play tricks. A gang of them would go out for liquid lunch, but they never invited Cello – same with the increasingly-frequent celebration nights – which were mostly down to his successes. I went on one lunch out – Never again. They were so coarse, crude, loud and obnoxious. I loathed them, but Cello never seemed to mind. I don't think he drank alcohol, anyway.

Sometimes he came and shared my Chinese lunch at the desk. 'Anytime,' I told him on several occasions, 'I always have spare chopsticks in my desk. and I invariably order more than I can eat.'

'Why?'

'So I can just dip into half-a-dozen different dishes instead of only two or three.'

One day, he didn't come in. 'Ring round everywhere,' the Big Boss was telling me. 'We have major deals on today. We need him in.'

I had a dozen numbers for him, but they were all dead or not answering. Everybody else started ringing them as well – they didn't believe me. But there was no sign of him. All day, the firm was in panic. The traders and whizzers were goggle-eyed and wide-open mouthed in dread as the realisation came to them. 'He's vanished, and all the firm's finances have gone with him.'

The boss sounded empty. Drained. 'We're looking into a deep, black pit of financial collapse.' The chaos and consternation had to be seen to be believed. Hair-tearing, raging, tears and bewilderment were the order of the day.

I lost nothing. He ring-fenced anything that I was involved with. Which wasn't much – I was mostly his gopher – go for this and that and anything else. 'See how we do this, Sheeela.

'Shred this and store that… skinny coffee and a dog with-a dill pickle…

'Will'a you phone my friend and tell her…? Buy a gift for… put this call through…

'How about you finish this deal, eh, mah deeer-a? Call this guy and tell him… file these…

'What's-a wrong with my cat? Check these numbers… have I made any spelling mistakes in this?

'Is that good grammar?'

He had actually emptied the firm's coffers – completely. Five separate trading accounts contained zilch – drained to numbered accounts that no-one was ever able to trace; they vanished somewhere the other side of Switzerland.

Obviously, I was in the top tier of suspects. A fortnight's questioning and accessing anything and everything I owned or had on my gadgets indicated that I had no idea what had happened. No more than anyone else, anyway. 'Nobody's that good at covering their tracks,' the police, my boss and my temporary solicitor agreed, and they turned me loose.

**

There was a note came the other day, a post-it in an envelope. "You fancee thee work for seex months in Hawaieee?" It really did say exactly that. And it was signed, "Cello. With no strings".

I just love the idea of working in Hawaii for six months. Big change from Philadelphia. I memorised the number on the post-it. I keep picking up the cell.

'Mmm, yesss,' I decide, 'I do eet. Now then, his number… Hawaii is Eight, Oh, Eight…'

THE NERD ON THE FERRY

'Coffee?' I said. 'This one's decaff and *this's* straight.' Blank eyes gazed up through circular wire-rim glasses in near shock at being spoken to. I repeated it, already regretting my rash decision to talk to him, but there really was no-one else aboard I could chatter with, no-one who was awake, anyway. All in their rooms or laid-out asleep in the lowerlounge.

Too late now. He took one. He had a weak little smile for a fleeting moment, then reverted to nerdsville. 'On your own?' I asked.

He nodded. 'You're alone, too, Miss… er…?'

'Only until we get to the island. I have family there.' We sipped the coffee. It was disgusting. An uncomfortable silence – why? I'm usually full of chat and stush. *Omigod, he's even nerdier close up, I've let myself in for it here. But it's not too late, I can drink the coffee, then clear off and leave him in his vacant mind.* 'You're not going to invite me to sit down?' *There – I've done it now – my mouth should never have said that.*

He had the nerve to look shocked, 'Er, yes, sure.' He casually waved a hand, and managed a feeble non-smile. *Lord, what have I done?* This duppy nerd went three shades paler, all nerves at being spoken to by a Whitney – black-and-smarter-than-you – as I like to think of myself when I'm in my smarticle mood.

'I've got cancer,' I told him; just to get his attention.

'No, you haven't.' He contradicted me flat, 'My wife had cancer. She *never* said it like that.' He sniffed at the coffee again.

73

Oh, Lord, what have I let myself in for? Only five minutes ago I'd been wandering, restless, aimless around the ferry's lounge area – big and bare, with easy-clean plastic seating and tables. I could have wiped the tables for more fun.

It was three in the morning and the place was dim, dead and empty. *Nobody* in there. Until I spied him – a white guy – a ghostie – staring uncomprehendingly into nowhere. He wore a high-vis bag on a high-vis strap diagonally across his chest. Lord, that spelled *total* nerd. Little round glasses.. Maybe I felt a bit sorry for him, sitting in a bare lounge with only his unbrushed mousey hair and a book for company. How can he sit and read, when we're heading for paradise! *My* Paradise – my *Tropical* Paradise. He sipped the coffee and looked at me – I'm fascinating like that, especially to a nerd like him. At least he was awake-ish, for all his pathetic look. It needn't be for long; he was someone to amuse myself with, to while away the night hours. These people, they just don't appreciate— never mind.

Here was me, all excited, going to take over the family business – The King's Resort. *I'm going home! I'm so excited. And no-one to share it with. I must tell someone.* It was a pity the only person to tell was a whogee wimp like him, but *someone* ought to know.

There was just this little niggle in my mind… It's a thing on the island: if you come back, you should bring more than you took away. I could see the interrogation now, 'So what have you brought, Chandice? Are you wealthy? Do you have great knowledge? Are you married to a rich and powerful man?'

Yes, the rest of the family was going to mount considerable opposition to me taking over if I wasn't bringing any particular skills, or putting my own money into the company. But Father had left it to me. Just me. Not them. He must have had a reason – he was never stupid. If my brothers and sisters opposed me, the workers would side with them. And, between them, they could outlast me.

All the way over here, I'd been racking my brain for the right angle on what I had to offer – something to convince them. But: I was broke; not married; not even got a feller these days. In fact, I didn't know anything real about running a hotel resort in the Caribbean.

Talking with this guy was catatonic. I must have been desperate. I never ever went up to a ghostie guy and chatted him up before, even all the time I've been in London. Business, yes, but never social. Looking at this guy now, never again. *Oh Boy, have I clanged.* He said hardly anything, but I was running my mouth off, like I do. 'You're especially white, even for a milky— You're *so* white, aren't you? How come? You been ill? Got something?' Of course, I know I shouldn't say things like that, but he was asking for it. Besides, this is *my* part of the world.

'It's called prison pallor. I've been in jail.' He was just saying it to get rid of me, I could tell, 'Three years. Out a month ago. Done my time.'

I had to laugh at the thought of a geeky pastaboy like him doing anything a millimetre out of line, 'Yes? What did you do? Kill your wife?'

That sorted him out, true enough. He went all eyes-down, nodded, 'Mmm.' Just for effect, I reckoned and I laughed again. Yes, I know it wasn't the most politic thing to do, but he was such an asking-for-it huti-rat. And the book he was reading – it was about *flowers*, for

75

Lordsake. Not even a decent lusty romance or crime thriller to get his rocks over. *Flowers!* Huh!

'Not very appropriate reading for a wife-killer, eh?' I flicked a hand at it. *Why do I always say things like that?* No wonder I stick with my own crowd in Harlesden. I reckon I only said it to get rid of him, but he stayed put. He was there first, I suppose.

'I suppose not,' he looked at the cover as if he hadn't realised before, 'but if I read a murder mystery, I just see myself as the hero killer and it spoils the effect the author wants.' The dead-eye look he gave me then, like he meant it!

I gave him a few more minutes of my wit, wisdom and island nous, but he was dead to it. I should have known I'd be wasting my time when I first spied him in his little niche.

In the end, it was me who backed off and left him to it. He had this irritating little smile at me, thanked me for my company. Sarcastic *gammon*. I gave him a farewell-and-never-again wiggle, and left him to his little book of blossoms.

 So we docked and I was met by the hotel jeep. An open bus picked up two or three dozen guests for the Resort.

The trouble started when I arrived at King's Resort. My little brother and sisters were dead against me being there, and weren't going to take my arrival the easy way. But the place was mine: I had the paperwork and the law on my side. Besides, they'd been letting it run down – probably syphoning-off for the past few months, since dad died. Yes, all resistance, they were, and ganging up as we looked round the place. *It's changed a lot since I was a little girl living here. Not the main buildings,*

they're much the same as I remember, but the guest rooms and beach cabins were refurbed around a year ago.

Showing me round the whole site, they were really getting on to me, 'What qualifications you got for taking over, Chandice?'

'What do you know about running a tropic hotel resort?'

'What you brought? Money to inject?'

'You the Priestess of Enterprise?'

After an hour or two of interrogation and scorning me, we were arriving back in Reception. *Oh, Lord, that irritating creature from the ferry.* Hovering round, trying to negotiate a cheap deal for a small single room, no service or food. He saw me. I stared back, giving him the hostile vibes, but he waved bone-white fingers at me; and smiled. I glowered back. My brother, Rolando saw, peering with suspicion at the hapless honk. My ferry-nightmare opened a plastic folder and counted some money, calculated something, and stated, 'As long as it costs less than a hundred dollars for three weeks... Oh. Well, how long can I have for a hundred dollars, then? *Two nights? Is that all?* I'll have to leave it.'

Gloria pointed him into town for a room. 'End of the drive. Left. Keep going.'

He turned to go, picking up his bag, eyes down. That little secret smile. *Not too put out at the refusal of a room, huh*? A nerd who's all eyes-down and quiet? I'm the opposite – eyes forward and all challenge – it's how I get my way. Everything else forward, too.

Indeed. This was Time to Control. I strode over to him, brushing my brother aside, 'We might as well cease the pretence, Genna,' I said, really loudly. 'They've rumbled us.' I grabbed his arm. 'Shut up,' I whispered.

77

'Not one word. Lots of smiles. *And stand up straight.*'
And led him forcibly to Rolando, standing there gob-smacked.

I do have to give him credit for that – he did exactly that. He got taller, and the smile morphed, straight into a typical snooty-pork smile, all supercilious. It was perfect.

'My fiancé,' I introduced Utter Nerd. I blushed inside to say it, and couldn't imagine any reality to it. 'He's the new Genna. You call him Genna. You do what he says, and me, what I say.'

I must have been mad to announce him as my General Manager, my Kingpin. It was desperate, sure enough. Of course, they're all total disbelief, until he's extracting a notebook from his bag and making notes as he stares round the foyer, and fixing his glass-adorned eyes onto each person in turn. And the way he loftily snoots over everybody, over his glasses and down his nose! He was like straight from one acting role to another without a breath.

Then they were into incredulity – believing it, without believing it. He was like something from Mary Poppins! And then! Then, he gets out an earpiece, sticks it in his juglug and starts talking like he's dictating about everybody. Boy! Did that shake'em awake!

He kept it up for half an hour... an hour... going all round. He ignored everybody's questions – put a finger to his lips to shut Rolando up. And even did that to Javier and Mirabelle and Susannah! He just looked at them – looked so *down* at them. It was absolute 'onk arrogance they got from him – and it worked perfectly.

Give him credit again: he didn't ask anything until we were alone in a suite. 'Okay, I know your name's Chandice, and that means "Clever Girl" – which I only know because there's an orchid called Chandice – I

78

learned a load of things about orchids in prison.' He looked round, like he wanted a drink or something. 'I think I get what's going on here, so what's the deal? Free board for me for, say, one month?'

'Okay, then I throw you out. I'm not having you parasiting round forever; let's get that clear from the start.'

'And what's included?'

'Everything.'

'Everything?' and looked at the bed.

'You think I'd... with *you?* Everything *else.' Yeuk – with him? Double yeuk.*

He had that irritating little smile again. 'Because I'm white?'

I stopped in mid retort... faced it, 'It ain't only that you're white – you're little, obnoxious, snooty, and you're *fish-belly* white. That enough?'

'Tell it how it is, huh? Okay,' He shrugged. 'I told you how I got so pasty. It's not too late to change your mind; tell'em you got cataracts, couldn't see me properly, and picked the wrong guy. Give me a twenty, local cash, for the time I put in already, and we'll call it quits.'

'You think I'm stupid?' I was really angry with him. 'You're going to be harder than I thought.'

'You didn't think at all, Chandice. So I will – This is the De Loren family, isn't it? Now then, I know a bit about you from the book.'

The book he had. It was the one my father wrote when I was a little girl – about the orchids on the island. I looked at it a long time ago. His copy was a different cover, but there was the write-up on my dad on the back, and he wrote things about the family inside when he talked about how he found some of the plants – seven

79

unique species of orchid. Including Chandice, that he named after me. 'I just thought it was only on the island that anybody knew that.'

'Maybe,' he says. 'But it's the standard reference on this island's orchids – the only one. So growers and breeders will have copies; societies, RHS library – that kind of place. It was the only book in prison that wasn't gangsters for my first few months, and I became interested. Studied all about it – orchids in general. Wrote to the publisher, in England, for info on it. They offered to pay half my costs for a month for a complete update on it.'

He had that weak little smile again, 'Except I didn't have the other half. But here I am, anyway, to explore the forests and gardens, get newer pictures and details.'

'You're like, *modernising* dad's book?' I wasn't sure about that, but he said it would still be in the name of Lawrence De Loren, but with him – my ghostie guy – alongside him on the back cover.

We agreed that we would both do our best to accommodate the other; and would not mess each other about. We left the "or else" bit unspoken. But I had my fingers crossed when I was agreeing to that – Like I'm going to be held to something by *him?* No chance, but I'd provide him with family updates and pics for the book, and let him talk with the grounds-staff.

'Did you really kill your wife?' Well, I had to ask, didn't I?

He didn't say anything for a minute, then he sat down and said, 'Yes, I did. Don't worry: you're safe, and nobody's after me: I done my time.'

'Like I'd be scared of *you?* So what happened?' I just got to know these things.

'Her cancer was getting really bad, painful. She was asleep one day when I got home early. She left a note. Maybe I could have got the emergency services there in time. But I stayed with her all night and felt her drift off, a last sigh. And I waited till daybreak.

'She was cold when they got to our house. They knew what I'd done and said it was murder. I pleaded guilty. Didn't want all about her pain coming out in a trial. I got four years, reduced to three. It was fair enough.' He shrugged, but no little smile, so I thought maybe he wasn't lying this time.

He was good! He spoke to the family and workers like he knew what he was doing. Both the resort management, people's jobs, the utilities and supplies – and the orchids and stuff. Never told them anything. Never answered anything. Just asked, like chattering. Talked into his ear-piece. Wrote in his notebook. Let slip things about the family, including details from long ago that he'd read in the book and his research in England about the orchids.

Rolando and Xavier couldn't decide if he was a conman or a gangster. 'He's a Samfy Man, Sister; you just found him somewhere on your travels. And you trying to wipe us up with him.'

'My Genna? He's a Qwenga alright,' I mocked them, 'Big rackets firm in London. He does the violent robbery thing – see how he's so white? Been in jail in England. Escaped. Convicted killer, he is. Look in his eyes – you'll see. You try crossing him and see how good he is with the seventeen-inch Imacasa he carries, eh?' That machete was a stroke of genius – a white guy sauntering round with a machete was so slave-days it was too real –

81

Rolando crossed him after about a week and the guy just swung the blade onto the table-top, right between his fingers!

'That was brilliant,' I told him afterwards.

'Accident,' he told me, 'It slipped out my grip.' But he had that annoying little smile again, and he took my hand and lifted it and kissed my knuckles.

That was so horrible! I nearly knuckled him back, but that skinny smile was still there. I think he sort of liked me. Yurk! It was reciprocated about as much as I adore rotted fish-guts. I had to remind him – at the point of a letter-opener – that this was a relationship of business convenience and *nothing else*. And he says, 'Ah, you say that, my love, but last night…'

I thought he was going to kiss my hand again, but he saw my look and he grinned. I was actually sick at the thought of anything happening between us, whether last night or any other. And if anyone believed it! That would be as bad. With his last breath, he said, 'But isn't that the whole idea, oh, My Beloved?'

That was about the turning point for us. My siblings and the staff and workers were all believing it. They were doing the work and doing what he suggested, and what I said, and behaving themselves. The hotel was running well.

I let it continue smoothly; getting itself into the efficiency groove; learning all the ropes and his tricks for myself.

'Chandice?' Anton turned to me one morning, 'considering the Genna is your betrothed, you never show him any affection? I can tell, from the little things you do, that you deep with him – tuned in, like – but you don't show it too much. You ought to. It looks like you made for each other. Don't need to hide it all the time.'

Oh? Do I? I can't. I mean, he's a... I can't let anything like that be seen... I don't think... I don't know...

I never took a real strong liking to a ghostie all the time I was in England, not sex-wise. And I certainly never mixed with them in deep-social situations, parties and such. Do I fantasise about him? Want to be with him? *I couldn't. I can't let him see that... Even if I do...*

Then Gloria says, kind of private-like, 'You're not even pretending you're engaged to him, Chandice. So if you are, I think you gonna lose him – I see how he looks at you sometimes; and I see the same from you. I think you need to tell each other, or you lose it.

'And if you're not pledged to be married, you should get on with it, and get pledged soon, cause that's what you need.'

'You mind your own, girl,' I told her. 'I know what I'm doing.'

But... I was still not knowing. I knew she was right about some of that, but I didn't know what to do. Maybe precipitate things...

'Genna,' I told him, 'You're not doing anything now – just wandering round with the earpiece, notebook and the Seventeen-incher swinging from your belt. So I'm feeling pretty secure now, and we won't have to put up with each other much longer. Just so you know, you're on notice.'

He looked at me, like stilled in his tracks. How the blue-faced booby can anyone manage such a tiny non-shrug, with, like half an eyebrow and a minimal pout?

83

'Just as long as you realise the position,' I told him. 'You'll be getting ready to be out soon.'

The evenings and nights were an embarrassment, a nightmare sometimes. I'd never spent an evening with a white guy before, much less a night. We had times in the common room with the family or the guests and put on the act; and he was casual, and the lies and stories just slipped off his tongue. Then we had times in my suite when I did the books or read The Islander; and he did the same and made notes about the orchids round the resort gardens, and was assembling pages and photos on his laptop. Even sent a first draft off to his publisher in London.

We slept in the same very big wide bed, for appearances when the room maids came in. But with the bolster down the middle, and a sheet that went over me and under him, so he needn't get any ideas like that.

One morning when I woke up, his hand was draped over my arm. I stared at the offending thing and poked him. 'Get that away at once,' I said and gave him the cold look.

He woke up and just chuckled at me! I pushed it off me and he sort of stroked my arm as it slipped away. Violated! 'Never do that again: it's most definitely not part of our arrangement. You're receiving B&B for nothing – it's not like you're doing anything nowadays – and it doesn't include any of *that* kind of thing.'

'You don't remember last night, then?' He had that same sneaky smile as he was getting out the bed, sliding his stupid glasses on.

'What! What?' I know I blushed. It came to me – I'd woken once and I had my arm across him; and I kept it there. It felt good, surprising me with such muscle and warmth. Not fishy and slippery like I always thought.

'You were awake? And you let me keep my hand on you? You gammon!' I was having flash-backs of more than that, but they were only dream-scenes, not real.

Then there was the day when we were walking through the gardens down to the staff village when I found I'd reached and taken his hand. After a minute he looked at me with that knowing little smile, and I blushed again, 'I wasn't thinking straight,' I told him. 'I got no excuse; by the time I realised, it didn't seem right to let go and shout at you. Not when other folk might be watching. Besides, you're carrying the Imacasa.'

'I released your hand when we came inside. It was you who took it up again. and it's not the only time we held hands.' He comes up with that damn smile, 'I quite liked it. Made me feel better. I thought you seemed okay with it, too. No?'

That was what decided it. *Him feeling close to me?* Oh, no. Getting close with him was not on my agenda. Even if I... a bit, maybe. I told him that night, 'Tomorrow. You're all done here. Don't need a genna any more. Tomorrow; you go.'

He looked at me like he expected more. 'It seems to be going well? You've haven't had me whipped for at least a week.'

That knowing little smile! 'That was the deal,' I said. 'The month must be up.'

He looked at me like he was going to say more, and he says, 'No, really, I thought... we've both said a few things recently... I thought we—'

'No!' The idea of any "we" was a shocker. I haven't been doing any ahead-thinking like that. 'Me and you? No way. Not on this God's sweet Earth.'

He gives me the dry smile back – never changed. Merely nodded, 'Near enough to a month, if that's how you want it.'

'Well, you've interviewed all the family and staff, and made notes and dictated into your earpiece and recorded everything. It's all done. I'm okay and I don't need you any more. Besides… here, you're an—'

'Yes, I am, aren't I?' He was turning his hands over, like checking the colour or something.

Damn him: he had me blushing again. It was always me who said the wrong things. But it needed saying. Before anything got further. Okay, so I was bound to say some wrong things – I was the only one who spoke most of the time. Damnit. He could hardly not be aware of my colour – I'm on the darker side of black – but he never said a word about it, like it really didn't make any difference in his mind or his eyes. He said one time he loved the fine carve of my lips… and the superb contrast in my eyes – like I was just a painting or something. When I insisted, he said my skin was Umber Glow.

'Like I want you talking about my skin,' I told him.

'I'll be gone, then, Chandice de Loren. By the way… my recordings and notes; interviews. They'll not be any use to you, I was just chatting and writing some background for the orchid book. The earpiece? It's music that I really missed inside – my iTunes player. I just mumble, or sing to myself a lot.'

'That was all a bluff?' I was gob-smacked *again*. 'Like the machete?'

He sighed and smiled that condescending smile, 'Of course. I used to be the manager of a small multi-materials engineering firm. I was pretty good, kept eight dozen guys and eighteen women in good and happy order. Lost my job, of course. I've only ever stayed in a hotel a couple of times; never one like this place.' He laughed, looked round, 'It's been good. 'I'll be gone in the morning, Petal.'

I blew up. 'You know I hate you calling me that: it's patronising and colonial and typical duppy… everything that's wrong with you.'

'Petal?' He pretended to think about it. 'Yes, you're right, Mz de Loren. I shouldn't. You said before. I'm sorry.'

He sort gave a little bow of apology. Nobody ever did that to me. That was respect; from a white man! Except he's a master of sarcasm, 'So why'd you do it? Why do you say things like that?' My mouth went the wrong direction again.

'It… I called my wife Petal. It was… like, I dunno, affection, I suppose.'

'That's the wife you murdered, is it?' God! My mouth! When it gets running, it goes full speed and there's no stopping it.

The look on his face! He died. He froze. He said nothing. Just stood there. Like he was dead.

I stared at him, like silent-ordering him to get out *now*. He looked wobbly. I never saw him like that before. 'You best go.' Then he was sort of shambling round and started collecting some things together, like deliberately taking his time and sing-mumbling some trashy tune to himself. He was always doing that. I caught the mumbles, '…sad to say, I'm on mi way… mi heart is down, mi head is turning around…'

Huh, he needn't come that. I left him to it; him and his gammon smile, '…had to leave a little girl in Kingston Town…'

We didn't speak again; didn't see him. Maybe he slept somewhere in the resort. But he was gone before first light.

What was I to think? My head spun at the speed of it. All empty. But it needed doing. It was done – he'd done nothing for a week, and not much before that. This was how I'd imagined it being: me in charge, on my own. Me the Genna. Yeah, this was a relief; I was rid of him. Bad influence on me and the staff and the family, too much like colonial *ofay* rule.

Dammit, within two days I was missing him like a thorn I'd become accustomed to; adjusted to. I mean, in bed – we never. But now I'm kinda missing it. Just being there close.

The day after that, I saw some slack room cleaning. Then I found the girls were taking time off instead of doing the work. The bar ran out of Don Papa rum and I couldn't get it at the same price, not in a rush. The phone was cut off and no-one arranged for the guy to come and fix it. The petrol store had been drained and nobody knew if it was stolen or just used up.

Rolando didn't come to my six o'clock meeting one day, and he was downright defiant when I told him off. Gloria said she was having a few days out with her new fella. And Damarcus the barman was definitely the worse for drink by midnight. It was Mirabelle and Susannah who were telling me about that, and a couple of things happening in the bar overnight.

'Yeah, okay, Suze, so I need to crack down on them.'

'I don't like to say, Chandice, but you need to work it like The Genna did, without saying anything, he just look sideways.'

'And he had the seventeen-inch Imacasa…'

'Yeah, y'right, Mirry. I know. But he's gone. The off-island ferry left a week ago. Must be in Port St. Pierre by now, or on the way to Newtown Prince, and that's a hundred kilometres away. Good riddance. Damn ghostie. I expect he'll be heading for New Castleton for his flight back to England.'

'Chandice?' Mirabelle had that confidential tone that meant she knew the big secret and was going to tell me. 'Maybe, if you wanted to know? The Genna's still on the island.'

'I don't.'

'Chandice?' She still had that tone, 'if you change your mind, somebody said he was still doing some of the orchid thing with his camera and little book part of the time, in the Creepy Forest past the Royal Gardens.'

'And he's sleeping in one of the surf shacks at White Shark Pier…'

'Yeah, he would be, wouldn't he?' Like I want to hear any of this. I'm done with him.

'Dajuan and Delyse saw him in FlotSam's Bar down Mango Beach. He was drinking with a couple of the beach girls and the surfing crowd.'

'Him? Surfing? Keeping out my way, more like.' *How dare he? Still here on my island. How's this gonna make me look? No wonder the staff's getting uppity.*

'He's not bothering nobody.'

'He's bothering me. He's got to go.'

He was in FlotSam's Bar when I went down there – not my kind of place at all. There he was, among all the fishing nets and barrels, stuffed fish, shark jaws and buoys; all fugged up on the stink of callaloo and hot peppered gully wash. Not to mention all the washed-up human flotsam and jetsam in there. He was sagged down on a sofa chair that was unstuffing itself, along with a skinny quadroon babe in a bikini and saffron skirt, and a griffy in splash skirt and white lace. *My Genna! In a place like this!*

'*This* is what you do? In *here*? Place like *this!* You were my Genna, and I find you *here?* I thought you were gone. Why aren't you gone?' He's drinking beer and rum – he never touched alcohol while he was at King's Resort. In camp shirt and shorts – orange hibiscus! Awful taste. And… and… everything. '*You!* Go away!' I ordered the beach whores out.

He tried to stop them, but they knew better. 'She's not going far; she's FlotSam's daughter. She lives here, and she's with Morgan Pete, the surf chief. Abigay's—'

'I don't care about your slut – her name or who she is or anything.'

'She's not—'

'She's what I say she is. What you doing here?' Among all this tramp-gear and rotting nets all over – dozen or more drinking themselves to oblivion – my genna! Here!

'Looking after the place – can't you tell?' That smile! I hate it – it says too much. Knows too much. 'Morgan's checking the wave break on the point; and Sam's gone looking for some extra gin they got in their shack store. So I'm in charge; we gonna have a conch stew and hard dough bread. That was mentioned in your father's book.'

'You're drunk! How could you?'

Big stupid grin. 'Easy,' he says to me, 'somebody fills a glass, or hands me a bottle. I lift it to my mouth. Drink. And just keep doing it. Simple. I drink a *lot*. It was something I really missed when I was inside. Lot of catching up to do. Music and hooch – twin delights. Sex, you learn to do without. But rhythm and booze—'

'Shut up shut up shut up you stupid creature! No wonder your wife killed herself... I... I...'

To the Pit with me! What am I doing? Totally horrified. What I'd said. Nothing I could do then. Too late. *Need to get him away from here. Just compounding my... my whatever... He's my genna. Shouldn't be like this. He's mine. Making me look worse while ever he stays on the island.* 'Just get out! Get off the island. You're not wanted here. You're a damn hon— Just get out! Go!'

I started to back off. Must have been twenty-odd faces my direction. I was crashing. 'What you all staring at? You want him round? Time you'd gone, ghostie.' Me and my mouth. But he's got to go. 'You can't be here – you're my genna.'

He didn't say anything, just looking over to the two slaggers hovering round the bar.

I'm out of there. Mad as Raging Rocko. And I'm stomping and cursing him, Damn scabber getting at me. Why in Hades don't I know anything I want?

I'm flouncing out of there and slamming round, and back to the King's and telling myself, and everybody, and they're all cowering or laughing, I don'no.

I get in my room – cold. On my own. Nobody there to smile at, or say something to. Not there to say how good the day was... no word about tomorrow... No-one to have near, and a little jest while we're eating, about something in the day that one of us said or did. It's coming to me: I've cocked this as far up as can be.

Damn tossing and cussing all rotten night. I don't give in. Never. *This what I want? You don' know what you want, girl.* Not this. *You've done dead the opposite of what you want... haven't you, girl? I don't know. He'll be gone if I... yeah, good. Out my head. No. That's not*

91

what I want. I screwed it all up. All the time, I'm fighting myself. He'll be gone any day now. This'll make him go faster – or he'll disappear over the west coast scene. This was my chance to... what? to keep him here? Do I want him here? Do I really want him gone? I just made sure of that. Why'd I fight him? He don't fight me. I'm fighting myself. Can't believe I feel like that about a white guy – Do I? I *can't.*

Shower. Lay some law out round the foyer, get them all told there's a new regime starting *now*. Sack Pitso in the bar. Shriek at the damn maids – they ought to be half-done with the rooms by now and get that rum in by noon or you're dead and if that computer's not back on line by the time I get back...

They're all edging right back out my way. And I don't know what I'm doing or going to say but I really deep down don't want this, how we are. I can *not* go on like this. Got to sort it. Sort him. What he really— What I really—

 'He don't sleep under the sofa no more.'

'He ain't here Chandeeece. Left in the night, after yo done all the shouting.'

'Finished his book notes few days ago... Relaxing round till the Port St. Pierre ferry, I reckon.'

'Din' say where he was going – back to his shack? – red-stripe, far end, I think.

God I am so ranting up. He's hiding from me? He just gone and left me? Just like that? What am I doing? I don' know. Gotta go and find him and get it sorted.

He's not damn here. Yeah – right shack – that's his old shirt. Prison shirt, he said. Nothing else. Damn him. Where's he gone hiding?

92

The guys round the shacks don't know. Just shrug. 'Who knows?'

'West beach? Some of'em going that way.'

'Big pipeline sea coming this week, they reckon. Maybe gone to catch that on Fraser's Reef.'

What's he damn doing to me? Why?

I went down Maurice Dock to check on boats out, 'No ferries till Thursday's, to MonCler.' So he an't gone. Kinda relieved.

'Some of the local boats'll take passengers across to Ste Honore – good surfing there.'

'Or there's the dive-boat that brings groups over from Porto Kildare – that takes loose passengers back sometimes.'

'There's a few that do circles round the island, too.

What? Damnit to Las Aves and back! I missed him? He's gone? I drove him out. What I told him. Front of everybody. God! are them lot at King's in for a rough load of shit for the foreseeable next. I got my temper up at them alright.

'An't seen any of the locals leaving this morning, though… and the dive boat's not even arrived yet.'

Yeah, right. He's not gone yet then. Still somewhere round the island. Moved shacks for the surfing, perhaps?'

'There's Yessie's livestock boat, Chandice. She takes passengers who don't mind sharing with a bunch of cattle – paddling in sea water and cow shit for a couple of hours over to MonCler.'

'Yeah – she's usually docked up somewhere near the launch ramp – they have to walk the livestock aboard, o' course.'

'Launch ramp? Over by the timber stacks?'

93

I'm going dashing round there. Got to find him. Livestock boat? No sign along the jetty… There's the loading ramp – lot of fresh dung and stink. There's an open boat just left. Fifty metres out. Cattle in the well of it. Engine just gunning up as they're getting near the rougher open water. That's him! Sitting on the back boarding looking out past the light tower.

I yelled and screamed and he didn't hear and I went running fast as I could along the harbour wall and I'm waving and yelling. Boat full of long-horns, tied together. Packed tight. The skipper up on the tiller hears me – sees me – says something. Genna looks up at her, turns to look my way.

He sees me, still running along the slabs past all the nets and bollards and fish boxes, and I'm stopping right on the end at the harbour entrance and yelling, and he's looking. And looking. And he don't move. He just looks at me.

I'm waving and yelling him to come back, come back and be my—

He's raising a hand, slow. Tiny wave, pale fingers. Stilled. He's looking. Fleeting little smile. He's turned away, hand slipping sideways, round the waist of someone half-hidden next to him. White lace top.

She snugs closer.

FOOTSIE

'Ladies and Gentlemen of the Press…' Ny Waterholes (Senior) paused for a moment whilst his impromptu audience quietened.

'Thank you for meeting with us here on the steps of the High Court this morning. You are clearly well aware of the mass of charges levelled against Dr Smith,' He indicated the gentleman beside him, 'by the police and CPS, the RSPCA, The Law Society, The Stock Exchange Regulatory Association, various *rag* newspapers – yourselves included – several television and radio news programmes, the Drug Abuse Council, and the whole of the Social Media from AndMe to ZoobyYou.

'I have been asked to speak on Dr Smith's behalf, as he says that, "If I get into a to-do with anyone then I'll effing murder the mad bee-stards." But he is not to be quoted on that.

'To outline our case: that day began, as many others do, with the cat jumping on the bed and attempting to nuzzle Mrs. Smith. She, in her semi-sleep, thought her husband was "trying it on", which he had been expressly forbidden to do on numerous occasions.'

He paused again as Dr Smith whispered to him. 'Indeed – Forbidden in no uncertain terms – witness Dr Smith's black eyes from the previous day.

'It is her claim that, in a violent, unthinking rage, she strangled Footsie before she was properly awake and became aware that it was not her lust-imbued husband.

'When she did realise what had occurred, she hurled the unfortunate cat out the window, and blamed her husband for setting the vicious, hateful little tabby on her. She proceeded to have a fit of the wobblies, and claimed that this was the last straw. She informed Dr Smith that she was definitely going ahead with the divorce which she had had been discussing with her solicitor for several weeks – on the grounds of his unreasonable behaviour. And her own unfaithfulness in playing footsy with, and I quote, "Everyone but the goalie," in the Nottdale United football team. Further, he was to sell all of their investment portfolio *immediately*, so that she could calculate her half, in preparation for her pending world cruise with The Goalie.

'As she was calming down, Dr Smith tried to reason with her.' Again, he paused as Dr Smith nodded and pointed to his neck brace. 'But she hit him several times over the head.

'He promptly telephoned his broker, with the words, and I quote, "Sell the whole effing lot, Josper. Everything. Yes, including the ISAs or whatever they're called these days. Yes, crystallise my losses… crystallise my balls for all I care. Yes. Now. At once. Immediately. She'll have it no other way."

'This, Ladies and Gentlemen, is a matter of record – all his phone calls are automatically recorded. This happened at 9.05 a.m. and the last of the transactions was finalised at 10.02 a.m.

'There was absolutely no way for Dr Smith to know that the stock market collapse would follow within the next half hour. This was, of course, due to many economic and political factors, nationally and internationally. There was also no possible way to know that one of the SE Detect and Response mechanisms is in the form of a particularly sensitive trading algorithm which was being tested on that quiet Tuesday morning. It is mooted that it

96

may be possible that this particular trade analysis algorithm over-reacted to a regular, medium-level investor who suddenly ditched all of his holdings in everything. Their own selling mechanisms were automatically brought into action, and this caused a widespread escalation among other brokers, who naturally monitor each other's trading. Sodds and Enders have yet to confirm that they *do* have a random group of fifty such investors whom their algo-trading mechanisms monitor in this way.

'They will, however, be obliged to admit this when they appear in court during these proceedings.

'Whatever the truth here, Dr Smith certainly had absolutely no awareness of this matter. He made no excessive profit whatsoever: he merely cashed in his investments at an obligatory moment. It was not a moment that he had intentionally created.

'He also has no knowledge of why his wife apparently dashed into the road whilst on her regular jogging run that afternoon.' The Honest Lawyer, as Ny Waterholes (Senior) liked to refer to himself, continued, 'Dr Smith has *never* accompanied her on a jogging run. As he says, "I'll go jogging when I see one of them silly miserable effers smiling."

'It is also recorded that Dr Smith was nowhere near Tooting Broadway at the time of the accident; he was being triaged in the A&E department of Queen's Hospital at 11.03, and was there until 17.30, receiving treatment for multiple abrasions and bruising; including the severe twisting of his neck that resulted in the need to wear the cervical collar.'

The pause on this occasion was purely for effect as the discomforted doctor eased the constriction around his throat. 'The police have not given appropriate consideration to the theory that Mrs Smith was overwrought by her row with the good doctor; or that she was wearing headphones and listening to motivational chanting when she ran onto the carriageway.

'The driver of the vehicle that collided with Mrs. Smith is facing charges of driving under the influence of drugs and/or alcohol. He and his eight passengers were returning home from an all-night party in Notting Hill. He has failed three separate blood tests. No-one in the vehicle was able to give a consistent or coherent account of Mrs Smith's death. There is no evidence whatsoever to suggest that Dr Smith had any acquaintance with the driver of the vehicle, or had paid him to kill his wife.

'He absolutely denies that he has ever supplied Mrs Smith with any dangerous, hallucinatory or illicit drugs. Nor even prescription medications – although obviously he is a doctor with some access to routine medical drugs. Nor does he know anyone who has unauthorised access to illegal or controlled drugs. No trace of drugs was found in Mrs. Smith's blood. Indeed, the police have not taken into account the fact that the person who first "came to her aid" whilst she was lying in the road was high on meth-amphetamine, was going through her purse, and has eleven convictions for drug manufacture. Dr Smith suggests that this person's clothes were saturated in various drugs, and that this is the reason traces were found on Mrs. Smith's body. And No – he did not pay the meth-man – known as "Tick Tick" – to push her into the path of the vehicle.

'And *No*, Dr Smith is not a cat-hater; nor has he had any affair with anyone since his wedding last year. He has no contacts in the stock exchange.

'The notion put forward by the police that he planned the whole matter, from persuading Footsy the cat to terrorise Mrs. Smith and trigger the divorce; thus bringing about the Footsie 100's biggest-ever one day fall; and then murdering her on Tooting Broadway in frustration – is simply untenable.

'All charges will be defended vigorously in court today.'

QUIZ NIGHT

The thump in my stomach was hard. Solid. Almost doubled me up, knocked me back. 'Errr.... Uffff...' Such force. So sudden, totally unexpected. Somebody really intended it. Rammed it into me. A knife. *I been stabbed.* This feller's got his fist in my belly. A knife right inside me. *Shit. What the hell for? That bloody hurts.*

He's short. He's fixed on me. His eyes staring into mine. Inches away as I sag forward and down. Blue. Pale flat blue eyes with pinpoint black dots. The lids clenched and I knew... The knife twisted, and tore upwards. Slicing inside me. So deep. *Shit, that hurts. This is serious.*

He was in the bar a few minutes ago. Looking round. Never seen him in the Brinsley Arms before. *This'll screw quiz night up.*

Maybe I pee'd myself. I dunno. Sinking. *My legs are losing it.*

Whafor? I was reaching for the door handle to get into the toilets, when it opened. He came out so quickly. Straight into me.

The knife's jerking upwards... almost lifting me off my feet. Again. *I feel wet... warm. That's blood...*

He's fading. I'm looking up at him now. He's staring down at me. So blue. Cold eyes. *Why?*

So cold. So dark. So utterly solidified cold. Frozen. Total darkness. Too cold to shiver.

I am nothing. Dead. I know I am. Time is passing... going by... Is this how it is? To be alone in the frozen darkness? *I bet the quiz was postponed. That'll have chalked off the opposition.*

Movement, so slight. Merely a vibration, a tiny sliding feeling. There's a lightness, blurred, starkness. I'm lying flat. A click. A jerking slide, headfirst. Someone is there. Low voices. 'Yes, that's her. May I be alone with her?'

The answer was slow coming, 'Okay. The cameras are on, though. Ten minutes?'

Silence again. A wait.

The voice again. Speaking to me? 'You can hear me? Yes, I feel you can. It was I who stabbed you with the knife. It was a mistake. I am terribly sorry for what I have done to you.'

It felt like he wanted an answer. What? From me? No way I could form any words – so cold and unmovingly solid.

'I was escaping some of my own people. Thought you were one of them. Expected you to be. I reacted... When I realised, it was too late to save you. You humans are so delicate. So easy to end you.'

He was over me somewhere in the blur – perhaps the smudge against the light? *I'm not truly hearing this?*

'I could not save you; not as a human. I could only lock your mind into your brain – not allow it to fade and fly. It is preserved. For a short time.'

I felt a touch on me... down my arm... chest... my stomach where I'd been torn open. So hard. It's me who's rigid. Frozen to rigidity. Am I crudely stitched up down there? Carved open for an autopsy? Like they have on the telly? Great criss-cross stitches? Someone having a last lingering look at my boobs?

'I can bring your mind into a body such as mine.'

Blue eyes? Short, stocky? I didn't say the words; that was all I recalled of the attacker. *How am I hearing this?*

'I can allow you – with great regret – to fade.'

To die?

The thoughts hesitated. 'We do not say that. It is a terrible thought for us.'

You did it to me.

'I have much remorse. I have come to make amends as much as I might. There is not long – do you wish to fade into the eternal consciousness, or be reborn into a body such as mine?'

How would I know? What are you like? You're not usually a dumpy little bald guy, are you?

I had a mental impression of…. Tentacles, claws flexing… a mass of hair-covered bulbous lumps…

That?

Or warm-cool nothingness?

'Er… what's the sex like with you lot?'

I CARE

A lonely part of the Yorkshire coast, I stood on the clifftop, empty inside, and put my phone away. There was a human body down there. *A human being!*

Half an hour ago, I'd been climbing up off the beach – very isolated, with only an overgrown footpath down the far end, so I'd scrambled up this way; no path, just picking a way between gorse bushes, brambles, miniature cliff faces where the clay had given way and slumped, forming treacherous pools of deep, soft mud.

I'd come across her, a girl – a young woman, almost completely buried in the hardened mud.

Stupidly, I felt my eyes stinging and I couldn't stop it. I was welling up and was glad no-one else was there to see it. Poor sod, buried in filthy sticky mud, with roots and insects over her... burrowing into her... Part-uncovered by cliff slippage and erosion.

I couldn't leave her like that. I couldn't. Not alone down there. The sea a hundred or so feet below her, buried in mud and rough grass. A few seagulls winging round.

It would be okay. The police would find me. I'd been very accurate is describing exactly where I was.

So I scrambled and slithered back down to be with her.

I just sat next to her in the deep grass and the clayey mud, still ninety percent buried, and thought I shouldn't clean her face – what was left of it – it would destroy any sort of evidence of anything there might be. But I was damned if I'd leave her alone, comfortless. I reached down to her, and held her hand... feeling the bones through

105

softened flesh. I held, and squeezed a little bit, as if it would comfort her.

'There's someone here. I'm with you now. You're not alone; you've been found; everything'll be okay now...

'Did you slip and fall? Walking alone? Or did the edge give way? Or did you walk into a pool of the sloppy clay? Tell me you weren't killed and dumped here? You're not alone; you've been found now; it'll all be well now.'

It seemed ages and ages as I sat with her and held her hand, a cold wind coming up off the sea, damp and chilling. I tried to talk with her, and look at that human face, so terribly destroyed; to say something of worth. But it all seemed so inadequate, so useless and I cursed myself for not doing better by her. Not even her name – so I thought of her as Sarah.

No-one passed by, not that I knew of – the path was back from the cliff edge just there, and I wouldn't have wanted anyone with us, anyway, intruding.

Then they were there, the police. Shouting from some distance away, and I shouted back and stood – I even said, 'Excuse me, Love,' when I let go of her hand.

They came down, a uniform and two beginner-police. They were all disbelief at first, until I held my hand out towards her, and they looked properly, and then woke up. The police girl was half-hysterical in tears and the other two weren't much better. The way they looked at me! Like I'd done it. *Guilt by being here,* I thought.

Well, they fussed about and pulled some more of the grass aside and I said, 'Should you be doing that without the forensics bods here?'

They got themselves together and went back to the top of the cliff for their mobile phone reception, and called it in. They said we should all leave the scene and wait on the cliff top and I said, 'No, I'm not leaving her alone again.

106

I'll wait here.' They tried to insist, but I refused, until their backup people arrived an hour later. Then I was okay to get out their way, and I went back up the top.

They didn't want to know me then. Just my name and address and phone number. And I was sent packing. A three-mile walk back along the cliffs to my car.

**

Three of them turned up on my doorstep two mornings later. All serious and accusatory. They wanted me to go to the station with them, and I wouldn't. They tried being threatening, then really obsequious. 'No,' I said. 'I don't like your tone. If you want to ask me things, we can do that here. If I come with you, you'll have to arrest me, and I won't say a single word that my solicitor hasn't passed for approval. No, I've got nothing to hide, I just don't like your attitude.'

The problem, it transpired, was that the girl's ring finger was missing. 'We know *you* cut it off, didn't you? Where is it? What did you do with her diamond ring?'

Idiots – they didn't know who she was, but were accusing me of stealing a ring they didn't even know existed. Just to rattle me, I suppose. That was when I did phone round and get myself a lawyer.

It made for a stupidly traumatic few weeks until the pathology lab determined that the finger had probably been removed at the time of death – probably two years ago, perhaps longer.

They seemed reluctant to tell me anything about her. Maybe embarrassment because they had no idea who she was. No-one locally had gone missing in the past five years. They'd collected all the so-called evidence from her body, and she would have a Pauper's Funeral, a Simple Council Funeral, I think they're called. A cremation on the cheap. They'd retain a tissue sample, for a possible DNA

107

profile before disposing of the body – God! So callous about it. But that was it. Finished.

I said I'd go to the service if they told me when. I'd pay for flowers, and take her ashes if they'd let me have them – scatter them somewhere nice.

**

'Any chance of a tissue sample or something?' I asked the youngster at Parson's Funeral Care. 'I'd like to see if I can find anything from her DNA profile.'

'Not a chance, officially' he told me. 'But there are sterile sample bottles in the cabinet there, and we don't count all the hairs and loose bits of flesh…' And he left the room for a ten-minute coffee break.

I sent the scraps to Ancestry.com and they came up with a sort of profile on her possible background area. I took it to the police and they said, 'Thank you. You should not have this. We'll look into it. There's the door. We'll contact you if there's anything new.'

**

Two months it took them. They matched her DNA profile to a young office worker in Leicester – 150 miles away. She'd been elimination-profiled as part of a robbery investigation at her place of work, along with a hundred other staff. They found her family and interviewed them. Apparently, she'd been going out with a local man, and they'd gone off for a weekend in London. 'Yeah, right – the London that's just north of Scarborough, eh?'

Her name was Marianne. She was twenty-two. 'Her parents won't see you or anyone else,' an officer told me. 'They've put it all behind them now. They're moving away but won't say where. We haven't been able to trace the man. We think he skipped the country not long after. Probably home in Portugal now. The investigation's open, but not active,' the inspector said. 'It's on the shelf.'

108

So are Marianne's ashes: they're on my mantel shelf. I think I'm the only one who cares.

I'M 86, YOU KNOW

I touched the button that lights up the little panel on the front door. It tells people I'm coming when they ring the bell. I'm not too quick sometimes, and I'm often in the room at the back of the house. It's called Kitchen.

I'm eighty-six, you know.

It was two people at the door. In dark uniforms.

Saying, 'Who are you?'

So I said, 'Why did you come here if you don't know who I am? And who are *you,* anyway?'

One of them must have been very impatient – I don't know which one. I was pushed aside and banged into the wall and they both came past me into my home. They didn't even ask. Or say who they were. So I said, 'I'm going to call the police.'

The runty little one came right up to me in my face and said, 'We *are* the police. So shut up.'

I think that one was a woman. It's hard to tell sometimes with the police. And she… it… pushed me back again and went back to the door and said, 'Your CCTV. We need to review the footage for the past two days.'

'You can't,' I told it.

It – By then, I'm fairly sure it's a woman, but not like any I ever knew – said, 'There's been an incident at number 16.

I said, 'That's across the road. I didn't see anything at all.'

The other one came back then. He'd been looking round the other rooms, and I never said he could. He didn't even ask. Policemen get younger and ruder these days. I'm eighty-three, you know.

He said, 'How do you know you haven't seen anything? We haven't said when it was or what it was.' The challenging tone of voice there!'

'I must ask you to go and sit down while we make checks.' The other one comes up with.

I told them I didn't want to sit down, 'I've only just stood up to answer the door, and after all that effort I might as well go the toilet while I'm up.' But he took my elbow and hustled me into the living room and made me sit down. Then he sat right in front of me and put his hands on my knees. I said, 'You shouldn't touch people like that.' And I tried to push his hands off my knees, but he gripped me hard and started to ask about across the road yesterday evening around eight o'clock, and did I see two men in hoodies? Or maybe three?

'No,' I said, 'I—'

'Are you sure? They'd be tall. Couple of white men? Perhaps carrying a large holdall? Do you know the girl across the road?'

'No. Which one?'

I thought he was going to jump down my throat, wanting to know, 'How can you say No you don't know her if you don't know which one I mean?'

I said, 'I know there are half a dozen or more kids on Roymead Close and some are girls, but I don't know any of them in a socio-recognition sense, or a biblical sense, or which houses they live in.'

'You're being evasive. You're lying, aren't you? What are you hiding' They were both on me then. 'You did see them, didn't you?' He was getting right in my face then and breathing on me, steaming up my glasses, and I'm eighty-eight, you know. And he's got hally-whatsit.

She starts demanding the footage from my outside camera. I tried to tell them they couldn't, but the big one, the definitely-a-man, got hold of my wrists and was pulling me and saying I was obstructing them, 'Is that how you want to play it?'

'How I want to play what? I don't play much of anything these days, except dominoes sometimes. I used to play around a lot. Golf, mostly.' But it was wasted on him.

The womanish one said I was letting the men get away with it. 'Is that what you want? You saw, didn't you? Or… or are you one of them?' She put on this really crafty-sounding voice. 'Are you in league with them? Maybe it was him, eh, Officer Runcival?'

'Like little girls, do you? Is that why—? Hello. And who are you?' He was up on his feet to face my newly-arriving visitor, all demanding and police-y.

'I'm Mathilda. I live here.'

That's my Matty, I thought, *just in time to save me.*

'You're rather young to be living with an old man, aren't you? What's going on here, then? Perverts, hmm? Both of you?'

Matty was behind me but I could tell she was furious. She gets like that. She ordered them out the house.

They wouldn't go. They arrested both of us and called some more police in to put handcuffs on us and said, 'You are to be charged with obstruction of an active police enquiry into the kidnap of a young girl.' Really theatrical, he was.

We were kept apart at the police station, and they tried to talk to me on my own, but I said, 'I'm eighty-five, you know, and I want a solicitor.' They always say that on the telly and they have to get you one and they tell you not to say anything.

'That proves you're hiding something.'

'We're applying for a warrant to search your house and take the CCTV recordings.'

'You already searched my house,' I said. 'That woman policeman went all round.'

He said, 'We'll do it properly this time and I wouldn't be surprised if *so much* gets broken...'

They did charge me with obstruction... 'and you will be held in custody while we pursue our enquiries and ascertain the level of your involvement.'

A solicitor who looked like an undertaker's assistant came in and said he had been allocated to me and he comes out with, 'They can do that. I'll speak with you in the morning.' He was useless. I hope I don't get him burying me when I pop my clogs. I'm eighty-four, you know. Not long to go. 'But they're just bluffing,' he said.

Or not – they did keep me there. And I didn't have my pills or my medication. I told them I needed it. Or my proper food. And no cocoa. Only one blanket, and I need wrapping up better than one blanket at my age. I'm eighty-seven you know.'

In the morning I was shivering. 'I need a proper toilet,' I told them; 'and my medication. And some proper clothes; you took mine off me.'

They escorted me to a clean room with a table and some chairs and I said again, 'I want my medication and some warm clothes and my solicitor.'

'All in good time,' one told me.

And that was when my Matty came in, 'This is Mr Beaks, your solicitor, Grandad.'

'Oh, yes?' I think I brightened up then – Matty and a real solicitor. 'Did you bring my medicine? And some food? I haven't eaten since breakfast yesterday. And a fire – I'm cold all through.'

114

They both said, 'Oh my God!' And they said the police had to go out while they talked to me. In private.

The police said I was in custody and had been charged.

'But not fed and watered,' I said. 'And I'm eighty-nine, you know.'

'Superintendent,' my Matty had her extra-patient voice on. 'Dr Bakersfield is aged ninety-four. Of course, he did not see anything across the road – He suffers from macular degeneration and is almost blind. He is diabetic and *needs* his medication. I am his grand-daughter. I have lived with him for three years, since my parents died in a traffic accident, and I look after him. Of course he said you can't have the CCTV footage: there isn't any. The camera's a plastic fake, a bluff.'

'We will be seeking,' Mr Beaks said, 'substantial damages for false arrest, the ill treatment he has received, and extensive damage caused to his property during unwarranted searches for unspecified items.'

'I believe the reporters outside this police station are from the BBC,' That was Matty's voice, 'and Sky News, and several newspapers.'

'Does that mean I'll be on the telly? I'm seventy-eight, you know, and I've never been on telly before.'

THE PRIM REAPER

I'm an honest young lady. Really. Now don't look at me like that.

I'm young. Ish.

A lady? Certainly. I'm polite to everyone.

I *am* honest, in the sense of fair and not cheating anybody.

I have not done any naughty things – that anyone knows of.

Okay, so I *have* done a few naughty-ish things, but not many people know about them.

Well, they know the things, but they don't know they were done by me.

I suppose *committed* by me would be fractionally more accurate, in that it conveys more of the mood, or sense of it.

My jobs are private. In lots of senses; I don't tell anyone. And they don't know who I am. People who know me would never believe it, anyway. And I'm not attached to anyone: I have no group or tribal loyalty, such as to a gang or a mob or anything like that. I'm independent. And I'll be naughty for anyone.

I receive referrals from time to time. Occasionally it's a phone call, text or email; but mostly it's a note or word from someone I've performed for previously.

I check my focus person before I accept a contract; I'm not going to kill just anyone. They might be really nice or a friend of mine. Not that I have any close friends.

I always vet the would-be contractor, too. Whoever they claim to be, or whoever someone else claims them to be, I check. They don't know me by sight. There's no pics of me anywhere. We never meet openly. They can't identify me at all. But I get to know them very well before I activate anything.

This one was everso very slightly awkward. Or these *two*, to be more correct. Two at once. Not unknown; no problem. I like to be busy; it keeps me on my toes, mentally speaking.

These two know each other – they nearly always do, obviously. It's why one of them wants the other one to be taking the ferry with Charon. I mean, I don't think I've ever pulled the curtains on someone who was a complete stranger to my employer. At my prices no-one is going to call time on someone they don't know.

The thing here with this one – these two – isn't that they know each other. But they've each offered me a card for the other one.

Over the past ten days, I find they're rival gang bosses – looking to become partners in a new merger, according to the very well-informed rumours down the Shamrock and Thistle.

It's a convenience that they dine together two nights a week. Like tonight. Here. In the Wallingdon Astor on Fremont and Fifth. So this is a great opportunity to size them both up. And, effectively decide which one to accept. I mean, I can't accept both contracts – I'd never be paid if they both joined the choir invisible.

Waitress uniforms here at the Wallingdon are available for a hundred bucks from the last girl going off duty. This one fits a treat – starchy, five foot three and trim like me. The bar is cluttered with trays or drinks with little labels for tables. So I stride round with a tray like I'm busy and study the pair of them from close to, or further away. And they call me over when I'm hovering. Perfect; to have them speak to me, I can balance their pros and cons better.

So up to them I trot, all prim and prissy as they all are in here. Bit of a surprise – I knew they were brothers, and I've seen photos, but for the life of me, I can't tell which is which. So I'm standing here slightly non-plussed, wondering.

One of them's asking if I'm okay. 'Something wrong young lady? You need to sit a moment?' He's all smiles and a touch of concern.

The other one's slipping his hand behind me and it's sliding up the back of my thigh and he's saying I can sit on his lap anytime, 'Like on my dick, eh?'

'If I can just put the tray down a moment, sir, if you wouldn't mind…'

So. Tray down. Kahr P.380 already in hand under the napkin. Two shots into his groin. Two to the belly. Two to the face. Fuck, was he surprised!

I bend to the other guy. 'You owe me a hundred grand. Mr, er?'

'Yellip.'

'I know that, which one?'

He caught on so damn quick. Too damn quick for his own good. Big smile. 'Ah,' he said, looking triumphant.

I'll not be getting my payout, will I?

I cotton on quick, too. I'm not having him piss me about. Sometimes you need to cut your losses. His steak knife through his left eye. Quick twist. Now

119

they've both got what they wanted. Word will get round. Business will be upped in the long term.

I need to hurry now. I'm out of here. And I'm running out shrieking in panic with all the others.

CONTENTS II

THIS NUN SMILED AT ME.

'That nun's smiling at you, dad.'

'Huh?' I tore myself away from the terms and conditions of getting a free coffee refill, and looked up. Sure enough. Twenty feet away, just like that, walking past in the café at the garden centre.

This nun's smiling at me. I did nothing to deserve that. Pity or reward, that's why nuns smile. We were just sitting there minding our own business, me and Julie and the kids.

I glanced back at my coffee and sausage roll, in case little fingers took a fancy to an extra nibble. She was definitely looking straight at me. She slowed and stopped and she smiled again. I mean – I hadn't smiled at her or anything. But I did then. Very weakly. Just being polite, I suppose. It's automatic to smile back at anyone. Even a nun. Even me.

Standing ten feet away, looking at me and smiling. I mean – a nun. It's unnerving – a fifty-year old virgin dressed up like Batman. Totally closed off from reality. Vacant mind that's utterly unaware of the world. Probably come looking for lost souls or pansies for the convent.

'Bob?' My missus muttered, 'who is she? You know her?'

'*No, I don't.* Like I'd know a nun. I don't want anything to do with'em. Religious nutters. She can look at somebody else with her silly smile.' I mean, how stupid do they come? Married to Christ my elbow. I saw that film, The Devils, so I know what nuns are like.

But she was still standing there. Came closer. Three feet away. Big happy smile like a toddler that's just managed on its potty for the first time. Bit puzzled, looking down at us.

'Robert?' she said. 'It *is* you.'

How does she know?

'I'm Alison, although I've been Sister Veronica for the past thirty years.'

'You're… Alison? Sis? *You?*'

'May I sit?' She was seated before I could nod or prevent. 'Are you going to introduce us?'

I remember that smile. I worshipped it at one time. Then hated it. 'My wife Julia… and Yvette, Mathilda and Geoffrey.'

'Bob?' Julia poked me.

'Alison. My sister.' I managed to wave a couple of dismissive fingers in that direction.

'Bob!' Julia had a short fuse. 'You never said you had a sister.' She could be quite accusatory, too. 'And what you looking so sour about? You should be delighted—'

'Alison abandoned me when I was seven. She smiled just like that, like she is now, the last time I saw her. Thirty years ago. Me seven, and her seventeen. Left me with dad, who carried on beating me up for the next ten years. I was miserable, bullied and in the gutter without a friend in the world. *I* couldn't run away and leave mum. *Like some people did.'* I gave my ex-sister-now-nun the dead eye.

She sat before me, a vision from a best-forgotten past – like something from Nightmare on Elm Street. Yes, it was the same face that walked out Number 36, all those years ago. Still that smile. I loathed it. It destroyed me that day; as she pulled the front door to behind her, just a big smile,

124

little wave. Gone. Just like that. Not a single word. I never saw her again. Until now.

'You joined up as a bloody nun? You deserted me and mum and took up religion? How could you? You know what hypocrisy is? Doesn't your conscience ever prick you? It should be stabbing you.'

I boiled... seethed... wanted to go. Felt my eyes stinging. There she sat, a beatific vision of peace and calm. How dare she turn up, all smile and fingers entwined.

'My child,' she said, her face lined like an ancient pear. 'My child, it is the way of God. He knew what was best for you and me.'

Yeeuuuukkkk! Sickening. Appalling. Complacent, know-all look that she'd always hid behind when I was a kid. Dad never touched her, not once. Too angelic-looking. Now that dreadful smile gazing at me again: the self-righteous face of a coward who'd looked after herself and buggered off to the comfy life.

It got to me. Bottled up, I blew – like a rocket on meth and speed. The table flew, the plates and cups went crashing away. Julia squawked; the kids yelled and fell away. Two almighty smacks across that face just felt *so* good.

I needed more. And a moment on, I was at her throat, the ungodly succubus – digging in and crushing deep. No laughing eyes now, they were wide in shock. And pain. I raved at her, the evil fiend. And tightened my grip to get her dead a-sap.

Lifting her up and ramming her down, her head crashing and thumping into the boards. She wouldn't smile and gloat and desert me again – the one I'd loved and trusted; and hated now with all my soul.

Someone was clawing at me, my face and head, my glasses gone. Pulling my mouth but it didn't hurt, and into my eyes. But I carried on and tore and crushed at her. An enormous blow hit my head. Another one. One smash more and my fingers weren't gripping... I was sinking down. Tried to grip deeper in sheer exploding hate...

All black and gone and I hoped she was dead, as I'd hoped so often before.

***

Some guy with a sixteen-inch ceramic plant pot had fractured my skull. Fractured? Shattered, it seems. I deserved it. I can't think straight, and everything's blurred. 'Guilty,' I told'em when the cops came round in the middle of visiting time, and warned me dire that I was looking at time galore in Wormwood Scrubs, for GBH.

'GBH? Is that all?' I mumbled thick. 'I was hoping for murder. Should have a medal for ridding the Earth of a demon soul, if you had the sense to see things right. That *kusipaa* is evil personified.'

'She can't speak yet—'

'Good – she's foul of mouth.'

'She indicates that she doesn't want to press charges.'

'Well I do. Can I charge myself? It shouldn't be up to her. It's in the public interest – let it all come out. Do me for attempted murder and her for endangering a child.'

'A child?'

'Me. Thirty years ago. Scarred me, it has. Ten years older than me, and she just cleared off.' I couldn't rant any more. I was spent and my head was dull and splitting again. I sagged back, 'That guy who stopped me should be charged with perverting the course of justice. She deserved to die.' That was it, run out of steam. Julia was there, looking concerned, but ready to take the other side.

126

'Give it a rest, mi duck,' I told her. 'I know, I know. I don't give a shit.'

Closing my eyes, not caring a jot what any of them does to me. I feel infinitely better than I have for thirty years.

GERONIMO!

'John Smith?'

I looked up at the call. Somebody at the door looking for me? The feller I was playing said, 'That's you she wants, is it?'

I shrugged, 'Don't know her. Come on, it's your go.' So I stayed focused on my pint and dominoes: they're the most important things in the Royal Tavern on Tuesday nights.

'Geronimo! I won!' Double four to finish. The old git looked a bit pissed, but he shook hands and stood to go back to his misery-gut mates. The Vinegar Arms lot are always sour sods.

Somebody was dropping into his seat. *Another loser fancying their chances, eh?*

'Eh?' It was her, the woman who'd stood at the door and announced my name. *Mmm, quite smart.* Near-black hair and eyes to match. *I wouldn't kick you out of bed, like, but...* 'Sorry, Love,' I said. 'I'm in the middle of a dominoes match against the Vinegars. Arch rivals, we are – neck and neck for the bottom spot this year. This's the cup, though; the final.

'You're John Smith?' She was smart, alright. Looked sharp-minded, *With the intellect and well as the figure and face, hmm?*

'Yes,' I admitted, vaguely hoping she was a nympho who had a fixation on men with my name. 'How did you know?'

'I didn't. You looked up.'

'So who the whatnot are you, some sort of spy? Matter-frigging-Harry?'

Her smile was a bit thin. She could have done better. 'You know I am.'

'Mrs Bond, I presume?' I even put on my Sean Connery accent – dead smooth. She looked blank. Silly girl. I shuffled the dominoes. 'You want a game?'

'You needn't pretend, John.'

'No, really, I'll play with you...' *If only – you're very smart.* I tried a sexy smile – you know, as lop-sided as I could manage, crooked eyebrows and all – James Bond style.

'Stop it, John Smith.' She was shuffling under the table. 'You're coming with me.'

Loosening your pants, eh? I decided. *I could come with you alright, mi duck.*

'I'll put a bullet through your gut in ten seconds, if you don't spark up. Don't think I won't. Look under the table.'

I dropped a domino – it's best to have a reason for bending down like that. Jeez! She did! No – not have loose pants on – she had a gun. Like a real one. With a long tube on the end. *Wow! A silencer.* Wouldn't really need it in there, what with all the cheering when Baggsy got a double-top finish on the dart board. There wasn't even a worthwhile view up her skirt – she had tight jeans on, the elastic sort that really cling. *This's the best prospect I've had since... well, since forever.*

'Four... three... two—'

'Where we going?' I knocked my little domino tower over.

'You know.'

I didn't. But I imagined the yard out the back would be a good starter. 'Maureen's Bike Shed,' as the landlord called it. It's the skittle alley, really, but Maureen uses it more than the skittles team. With more joy, I hear. 'You know about the alley, then? Just a quickie to start the night of passion off right, eh?'

She was looking a mite cross-eyed at the promise of that, but I reckon she was coming round to my point of view, except her eyes were turning upwards, over my head, *She's gone unfocused in her desire*, I decided. Except there was a tap on my shoulder – no, not that sort of tap – somebody's poking finger. *Some vinegary toe-rag wanting to pick an argument about sandwiches?* I supposed... *or trying to muscle in on Tight-Pants?*

'*I'm* John Smith,' comes this voice from, like three feet above and behind me. I twisted to look up, just enough of a scowl to be threatening and challenging – you know, like him in Silence of the Lambs. Yeah, this guy looked puzzled, face peering from her to me, a bit desperate.

'Piss off, I'm well in here,' I told him.

He starts knocking me round my head... pulling at me.

'Gerroff.'

But he's twice my size, and she's staying neutral. Looked a touch baffled, actually. *Obviously prefers me*, I reckoned, *but she dun't like to say*.

'Take your turn,' I'm saying, 'it's rude to interrupt.'

But he's dragging me away, and he's got a bloody gun, too. It's stuck up in my armpit. And he's dragging me out the back and towards the skittle alley down the side. 'I'm not going in there on mi own,' I told him. 'Not with you.' I was imagining all sorts.

But she's followed, and he's turning, and snapping at her, 'You've made us late, Luciana. 'Come on; we need to get a move on now.' I could tell she din't like being spoken to in that manner by a fart like him, but, as I said, he's twice my size, he's got a gun, and my cribbage game was next on, so I just watched as they went dashing across

131

the car park, scrambling into a Maserati... *a bloody Maserati! In the Royal! And still got all four wheels on it!*

'You're better off with me, duck,' I shouted after them, 'I've got a Ford. More reliable.'

You should see the tyre marks they left, nearly spinning into the main road. *Off to do some shooting and spying, I expect.*

So it was back in the pub for me, staying cool and calm, if a mite dishevelled. Coming the Hugh Grant bit – all innocent little boy style, 'Dumped for a sodding Maserati, just when we were getting on so well,' I mumbled philosophically to the room in general. 'Good job, really: having it off with her in the middle of DD and Crib Night would only put me off my game.'

Course, they were going to do some ribbing – like a pack of Frogs round the guillotine, they are. Pack of armoles, then the other guys finished their dominoes games and we started the cribbage. This was Champions Night, and we'd finish up with the second half of the darts match – at which we are the Ace Team.

I'm crap at cribbage – only been playing a couple of months, but we're short of players – and I got hammered two games to one. 'And one for his knob,' the grinning old git announced as he triumphantly moved the marker along the board and into the hole.

'I'll have you in the darts,' I told him as we shook hands, all gentleman-like.

There's always quiet for the darts, of course. A murmur of conversation from the far side, or somebody at the bar is all. Soddit – the old git was inspired. A one-sixty and a one-five-seven left him needing double top with three arrers. And I need one-four-eight.

Right, I was feeling a bit dead inside. Yeah, it's gettable. But with stakes like that night – Cup Night – my legs were shaking like summat that Ann Summers rep brought in once. I had a condemned-man sort of last sup of my bitter, and tried to ignore the muted calls of support. *Get focused, Johnny-Boy... Come on.*

I approached the oche. Door opened, six foot to my left. *I could make a dash for it* – my heart was ramming away. *No. Got to face this.* The silence descended. All eyes fixed on me and the dartboard.

I'm just settling my stance, shuffling, weighing up the first dart, focusing on treble sixteen. And I'm trembling like that washplant in Gold Rush.

'What model of Ford?'

All eyes swivelled doorwards, pints lowering, aghast at the interruption. It's her come back. Fixed smile. Still a bit thin.

'Eh?'

She repeated it. Every bugger looking, heads going like Wimbledon between us.

'Edge Estate. Room for a skittle alley in the back. You'd be alright in there.' *This's putting me off my game.*

'Edge?' That brightened her up a touch. 'Come on, John – get on with it. Get your priorities right...' I wondered exactly what she meant by that... imagination running wild as I checked my "priorities". But all the others were getting on at me, too.

I'm thinking like Drake – get the game finished, there's plenty of time to sort the Spaniard out. She did look a touch Spanish – near-black hair, high sheen to it. And her name was Lucy Arna, was it? Sounded foreign.

I measured up, steady as a rock, eyes seeing nothing else but treble sixteen... Yes!

Now treble top... Get in there!

And double top...

The Royal Tavern erupted.

It took two minutes to get to her, but, flushed and cool, I offered her a drink. She smiled again – it was quite nice – and I asked about her posh-car friend.

'He ran out of… well, everything, really – mostly pzazz and petrol. He's parked in the middle of Phoenix Roundabout.'

The drink was quick. She wanted more. No, not drink. Not the skittle alley, either. Or with the back down in the car. 'We have to do a job tonight. It'll have to be you. Can you handle a gun?' I felt a mite cross-eyed at the thought. 'Well,' she sleuthed out the corner of her mouth, all spy-like, 'You'll have to handle the gun or the car, and you're too drunk to drive.'

'I'm less of a risk with a gun, eh? Let's have a look; there's a safety something, isn't there?' I've heard about guns.

'I'll show you on the way. Now, we must get a move on. Fast.'

'And that Sirs, is basically how I got roped into it.' I gazed around the four of them, all in suits and grim expressions. Disbelieving lot. 'We won, din't we?' I said. 'Got the stuff? Didn't need to shoot anybody. She said that made it a successful mission.' *I did try to shoot somebody, but missed. It put the frighteners on 'em, though.* 'Er, she will be okay, will she? Lucy Whatnot? It was entirely her own fault; well, not mine, anyway.'

They give me the hard look, grim-like, like they got no choice, and one of 'em's going, 'We have little choice, Oh-oh-forty.'

'Hey,' I says, 'Oh-oh-double top? That'll do me. Wait till I tell 'em back in the Royal, they'll never believe… it'll look good on the dominoes sheet when we sign in, won't it?'

You know that kind of despairing look some people get? Well, this lot had it in spades, and one of them was saying, 'I think we have no choice, gentlemen.'

'Is he really all that's available?'

'He did handle the gun rather deftly…'

'The whole sagging situation, actually…'

'Well, Mr Smith…'

And that's how I was offered my second assignment for MI5 or whoever – they still won't tell me who I do these odd jobs for.

NOT MY MIRROR

'Guys! Please... *please...* Not in here... No fighting. It's a bar, not a cage.'

'Keep yer head down, Dorris,' O'Coyd yelled at me as he renewed his attack on that scrubby little Macky off Yard Street. But they were at it, both of'em getting stuck in, fists and knees everywhere.

'Guys!' *Especially not with...* 'Oh, come on, guys. No! you'll wreck my place. Guys, *please...*'

Macky grabbed the tapas dish holder – that went hurling away. And O'Coyd's scrabbling at the bottle rack.

'No, No! Not the bottles! No throwing. Y' doing it on purpose!'

One went flying.

'The mirror!!! Not the mirror!' A bottle flew. Arcing across the room.

The mirror went. My big beautiful expensive mirror. Huge silvery slivers of glass coming down in a shatter-storm across the floor. Fetching half the bottle display down with it. *Oh, shit... My insurance'll never believe this.*

The big round table gave way under their weight. 'No no. Noooo. Guys, you gotta stop it – not in here. Don't smash my bar up. Noooo...'

That big ginger bastard O'Coyd ranted and swung and obviously didn't care what he hit – half of it was trying to intimidate Whacky Macky by smashing anything near – as well as Macky's head. Except everything near belonged to me – *My* gin bar – open for a month. Cost me a fortune.

Nothing like as big as O'Coyd, but Macky was fast, nasty and clever, intent on beating the crap out of him since the moment he'd come stomping in and started it all off. Right in middle of a peaceful Friday evening when the place had filled-up nicely with happy punters on the bevvy.

Now they've all scarpered – they sure didn't want to know. You know how they'll be, don't you? Witness? Me, Officer? Never saw a thing… I was never there. And they aren't, not now. They're all half a mile away in record time.

Not me. I'm damned if I'm leaving my bar to the likes of these maniacs with a gangland grudge against each other – whatever. Probably an imagined past double-cross or something else they made up. Pair of thug-shits.

**

My mockup gin still in the centre of the room – an edifice of copper, brass and glass! They're rolling and staggering and dragging each other and colliding into it. Down it comes in a massive clanking clatter of copper and brass. Shiny metal and glass pressure dials crashing away in a me-shattering cacophony. And they went yelling and thumping, grunting and dragging each other across the wreckage. My whole bar – all battered-up. 'No, no. Nooooo. Not my still…' I was furious-wailing by then.

Rolling round on the floor in the glass and slops. Two-man pandemonium, it was. Two-mandemonium, I suppose. Macky's flat on his back and pinned down. Ginger O'Coyd's got a broke bottle by the neck in one hand, and Macky by the neck in the other. Going into Macky's face, carving him like he deserves. Both ranting like they were mad. Macky trying to fend him off – face a mass of cuts – deep ones – and brilliant blood. All splattering across my lovely new parquet floor. I wanted a few gin stains there, to make the place look snug, not *this*…

138

O'Coyd's easing back, kneeling on him hard down. *Won!* Snarling and still ranting and dishing out the threats. I dashed over there, begging him to stop it. 'Let him up, O'Cee... Leave my place alone... You done enough.'

Wa'n't going to. He whipped round – Effing ugly face. Big bastard, even on his knees. *But fast.* Slashed across my cheek. Bugger near had my eye out.

I just lost it. *This's my bar! My face!*

I saw the bottle base right there. Jagged spikes of razor-sharp glass. It threw itself into my hand, fingers clenching round it. O'Coyd's turned back to Bloodface Macky., snarling at him That bottle base twisted on its own. It rammed, all by itself. Right into his effing throat. Twisting. Deep. And the look! Surprise? Total disbelief, more like. But in it went. Hard and ramming. He sagged. Utter-shocked. He wa'n't believing it. Toppling down flat and clutching himself, on top of Shitehawk Macky.

Shit. You bleed out so sodding fast with your throat slashed open. And you can't do nothing about it with somebody kneeling in the middle of your back to keep you down. Even if it's only somebody my size.

Flat on his back, Macky couldn't move an inch, pinned down under O'Coyd. He was staring up, not seeing much, with all the blood puddling in his eyes. And sure not going anywhere with me on top of them both.

Stuffit, I scrabbled for the bloody bottle – the top end – out O'Coyd's no-longer-grasping grasp. 'Stuff you, too, Whacky.' And his throat got the same treatment with the top half of the bottle...

**

I was still lying there on top of them both when the rescue squad came in. The drinkers who'd not gone too far. They came in all timid and reticent at first, and I stayed down, pretending to be nearly passed-out. I knew precisely what

139

was going on. Maybe I'd lost a pint or so of blood, but I had my hand over my cheek, and that seemed to have stemmed the bleeding okay by the time I felt one of them lifting me up, and saw some of the others attempting to pull O'Coyd off Macky.

Finding they're both dead. Pulling the broken bottle halves out of'em. Checking pulses… How wonderful: they, all of them, were contaminating the crime scene. Paddling through the blood and gin – I saw a few bottles being spirited into pockets and handbags. *So you ain't gonna be the most reliable witnesses, are you? If you even stay that long.* There'll be so many sets of prints and DNA on the glassware the bobbies and bones lots'll never sort it out. It'll be so obvious that these two vicious shits had killed each other. I mean, who else could it have been? I'd tried to stop them. Courageously attempting to pull them apart. Got slashed for my trouble.

No witnesses. I was the only other one there at the time. Little Miss Dorris. Respectable owner of Dorris Ginn's Bar and Stillery. Sixty-three years of age. Wide-eyed and innocent. Five foot-two. Seven stone seven. Spotlessly clean record.

And a very nasty temper.

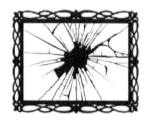

THE YULI ACCORD

It's that slight formal bow my Korean friends have, accompanied by *'Yeong-yeui yeoin.'* I smile around their little sea of suited managers' faces all looking up at me, and I do a formal nod and bow in return. Nice, that.

'Yeong-yeui yeoin? It's an honourable title, equivalent to *ajeossi,* even though you are a woman, not a respected middle aged gentleman,' Ji-hoon, my aide told me, back when, on my first-ever visit over here. 'It truly does denote their high esteem and great respect for you.'

'You wouldn't know it, the way they've screwed-up my designs and specifications,' I tell him these days. 'It's a wonder the structure is still vertical.' It's been a battle between me and my design, versus them and their cheap-skating, corner-cutting ways ever since.

So this time, I'm attending another site inspection and management meeting in Korea. As always, it's about the plans for the architectural feature in the parkland grounds of the prestigious glass corporation, *Yuli Gongsa.* I'm the architect, the designer, and they *are* polite and respectful to me most of the time.

Perhaps it's because I'm a good bit taller and broader than them, but it's mostly because they very much value my unique design for the Mister Whippy-style Ice Cream twirl in their park. Their very generous fee demonstrates their appreciation rather well, too. My structure is made of glass and stainless steel, is eight storeys high, and I am very proud of it. It will look magnificent in this sunlit situation, and on my CV. So it is doubly essential that it be right.

I drew up the original plans, and adapted them to the Yuli company's situation and specific requirements. I go out there every month to work with them, interpret aspects and check mutual understanding. I think they're getting to their budget limit, what with all the bribery that everybody else seems to be getting, so half the time they're testing what they might get away with, stress-toleration and building-inspectorate-wise. They want their Glass Palace, their Yuli Gungjeon on the cheap. 'It ain't gonna happen,' I told Jihoon.

My plans require high grade materials – surpassing their low-standard basic. Now, I'm no stainless steel expert in the general run of life, but the strength requirements for my sculptured-glass structure are high, both for the material itself and for the structure. It took yonks with the sims and models to get the right balance for the twisting curves for their several-times altered requirements. But I need recurving pre-stress beams of 11xx+ carbon steel. *'And nothing less.'*

But there they were, attempting to get away with an inferior grade of steel, and miss out one in six of the cross-bracing spars. I couldn't let it go. A decent wind – anything over sixty-five knots – and the frame would twist – the glass corkscrew would actually bend laterally and collapse in a spin. They *must* have all the braces and links in. Their re-calculations were hopelessly optimistic – in a country that averages seven typhoons a year – tropical storms, cyclones, whatever you want to call them.

142

This particular time, I was inspecting the main sheet glass panels for the exterior on the third level of the spiral – and it needed to be a sight better than the stuff they were fitting – sheets two mill thinner than requirements; it wasn't triple laminated; the expansion joints were a millimetre off – too big, or too tight – on most panels – and the glass just wouldn't give the degree of rigidity to the structure that was needed. I'd seen flaws in two panels already – they showed very clearly with the slight twisting in the light.

'Yuli is a glass manufacturer, for Gawd's sake, and you should know these things inside-out.' So I insisted that we meet to discuss my report in the Boss's *Samusil Seuwiteu* on the tenth floor. That's his ultra-posh suite that looks down on the parkland with marvellous views over the town as well as down onto my rising glass spiral. It really did look an absolute vision from up there. *Yuli Gijeog*, the locals were calling it – the Glass Miracle.

So I was invited to outline my objections to this latest endeavour on their part to cut corners on the costs and quality of the materials. 'It is mere trimming of corners,' they said. 'Of no detriment.'

'It's of detriment to me; my reputation.' I told them, very huffily, on my high horse.

So Kim Lideo, chief of construction gets up as soon as I finished, face like a plate of *kimchu* pickled cabbage, bows to me and thanks me for my words of wisdom. He then adds *Nyeon Chong-Nom* to my name. That's like "Designer Mary, *Punk-bitch bumpkin*" – and hawks up a great dollop of throat-clearing – as Korean men do – and gobbed straight towards me. Okay, so it missed by ten feet, but it was the principle of the action.

And he stood there, hardly coming up to my tits, with this insulting, challenging stare on his wizened ugly, toadlike, face.

They do that kind of spitting thing as a ritual; it's virtually routine for them.

However, 'I am the flower of Australian Womanhood, and I do not take *that* from you, you runty little goblin.' I grabbed his lapels, lifted him up and swung him against the wall to have serious words about you don't insult the bloom of The Antipodes in that manner – or any other manner – and get away with it.

It illustrated my point exactly: it was a glass wall.

It gave way when I slammed the little shit against it. The whole panel just collapsed in a mass of four-millimetre cubes and he went flying through.

Ten floors up, it took him 3.7 seconds to reach the ground. Plenty long enough to reflect on his cheap-skating ways with *this* building, too.

**

I suppose it's fortunate that the *Yuli Gongsa* company doesn't want to lose face.

We have this compromise now, an Agreement. I have it in my log as The Yuli Accord. They will stick exactly to my design requirements in future. They will continue with their story that Mr Kim committed suicide for no known reason, other than being fearful that his giving and receiving of bribes for contract materials was about to be disclosed. Courageous Lady tried to grab him in order to save him – apparently – they have such bravery, these Western Women. And they won't indulge in any more spitting in my presence.

For my part, I will not mention the quality of the glass in their headquarters; and I will not accidently throw anyone else out the window.

I'm not sure if they entirely trust me, though: all our meetings are now held in the ground floor Foyer Office.

THREE SILVER BUTTONS

Just wandering round the stalls on the flea market. Bitter cold day in a breeze that swirled round the stalls and corners of the moot hall. Everybody is heads-down into the biting wind – as much as anything to keep the bursts of sleet out their eyes. Chesterfield Market is especially good for two stalls selling ancient coins – which was what I mainly come for. Where they obtain such superb Greek and Celtic coins, I don't know – they won't say. But I've had them checked-out, and they're genuine, with believable provenance. *Must be from one of the big London or Birmingham dealers*, I reckon.

There are also some very good post-medieval British ones. And a terrific little stall that has classical books and rare poetry editions. And I like to browse the stalls buried under every workshop tool you could wish for. Every tool *I* could wish for, anyway; plus farm produce like duck eggs and bacon-wrapped chickens. Yes, my kind of delve-around market. *Not especially so on a day like this, though.*

Some stallholders hadn't turned up, people standing around for a blustery chatter, blocking the way, oblivious. I'm going, head down into the lashing gusts, glancing up into the wind. A woman so close. Striding towards me. A flash of eye contact, as if of recognition. Instant smile, both of us. Realisation that we're total strangers, the smiles slowing; a slight nod; and we'd passed each other – unknown to each other again. The fleeting vision – a second at most – was gone forever.

Except. My mind's eye retained an image of her. So detailed. So clear. Young. Fresh-scrubbed face. Clear blue-grey eyes. Minimal make-up – just the eye-lashes, maybe. Swept-back blonde hair tucked into a black hat, not much bigger than a fascinator, hardly the apparel for weather like this. Charcoal waist-coat-style jacket with three silver buttons; pencil skirt, slender legs... Shoes? Must have been. Didn't notice.

Another wet and icy blast. I sheltered among the garments stalls. *There's no way I'm staying outdoors for the whole morning; time to warm up. Wait for a lull, then head for the café.*

Oh, yes, she had a small black leather handbag over her left shoulder, my memory played back – so clear. We had each taken a fractional swerve to the right without breaking stride. And the smile. Warming. I hadn't turned to look; an already-vanished ship in the night. Except in the mind.

The longed-for lull in a series of swirling sleet gusts, and I checked out the last row of stalls, then headed for the café where they do the specials – tea or coffee with a choice of anything from the rolls and scones counter. All for three-fifty.

There was some hold-up at the front of the queue. But there were two servers on, so it was okay; we edged forward. The couple in front of me only wanted one scone to share with their two teas – which was the same price as one each. Then I shuffled up. Maisie-behind-the-counter knew me, 'Hi, Mr Gordano. Well today? The usual?'

I said something back and nodded and felt in my pockets for where I'd put the right money – they're always short of change.

It was *her*. At the front, with the other server – Gladys, I think she is. Standing there. Smile gone. Worried, she didn't know what to do. I sort of caught her eye, half-raised a hand in salutation – immediate recognition of that split-second's eye contact. 'Trouble?'

'My purse. It was in here.' Her handbag. 'I… I ordered cappuccino with After-Eights. I can't pay for it.'

'Please. Allow me, I'm fabulously wealthy. That's what I tell the ladies, anyway.'

The amazing, gorgeous smile that laughed, then froze and faded, 'I couldn't.'

'Of course you could. It's that or forsake your After Eights.' Such clear eyes.

That smile again – a bit weak, bit sad? 'I'll pay you back.'

'A smile like yours? You already have.' *You are beautiful. Stop staring, Roméo.*

Maisie-behind-the-counter was ear-wigging. 'Put her down, Mr Gordano.'

'Maisie always says that if I speak to anyone, including Olive – that's her cat, over there.'

So I collected my cup and plate, and sat in my usual place, well away from the door. A moment later, she joined me. 'Why?'

'Why what? Splash out some small change? It's nothing.' But she still wanted to know, so I tried to rationalise the spur of a moment. 'One – I was a boy scout – good deed and all that. Two – *I* haven't lost my money. And three – your smile – out there round the market? That has to be the best two quid I've ever spent – you got me there. My turn to smile – felt like I'd opened my stupid heart.

She blushed. It was lovely to see – such delicate colour. Eye-lashes fluttering down. 'People don't usually want to know me. They don't like me. Not… when they get to know me. Especially at work.'

'So: you're either in charge in a difficult job, and it's best not to get close. Or maybe you let them get to know the wrong You?'

She was quiet, sipped her cappuccino, nibbled at the mint chocolate. Three silver buttons so neatly set down the front of her near-black jacket; each with a coat of arms. 'I can't help who I am.'

'Almost true. You can't help who you *were* – right up to the present. But you *can* change who you are *now*. Fresh start this minute. You can do that any time.' I sipped my cuppa – the finest Yorkshire Tea in Chesterfield.

Fallen silent, she was thinking about it. Or simply dismissing me, having felt obliged to join me.

'Besides,' God, I'd be so embarrassed to say it… 'besides, you seem pretty much perfect to me.'

Eyelashes lifted a moment to meet my tremulous tenth-of-a-smile; and lowered again.

We sipped and nibbled and didn't talk much. Such a lovely face. Stunning. So elegant. She knew I was looking at her, appraising her. I tried not to, *but you are just so striking.* She radiated *nice.* 'Can you get home? You have a car? Bus fare? Whatever?'

'I'm okay. I have a car. A sporty Merc.' A smile that I wished was for me instead of some metallic hunk.

'Sports? An SL? AMG?'

'I wish.'

'The car park? Paying?'

Face panicked, 'Oh, God. No.'

'Here. Have a tenner. No, no, it's fine.'

She took it. A shy, embarrassed smile. 'Are you in here next week, Mr, er… Gordano?'

'Most weeks, around this time. But, if you come, don't even think about paying me back. I'm Roméo, by the way. Roméo Gordano.'

'Giulietta,' she said. That smile again. 'I *will* be back next week. My turn for the cappuccini.'

She slid out her seat and strode to the door, reaching for her phone to report her missing cards. Very smart lady. A few years older than me, maybe? The upper side of mid-twenties? So trim.

I really do hope she comes back next week. If only for another cappuccino – Or cappucci*ni,* as she said. *Speaks Italian, does she?*

I could feel myself sighing, 'Hi ho… la signorina è *molto* bella.'

Reaching into my pocket, I felt over the smooth leather surface. 'Now, before next Thursday, how can I get this purse back to her, complete with all its contents?'

THE PRY MINTSER

It was a big honour, everybody kept telling me, to meet the pry mintser when he came to school. I would meet him and shake hands and it was an honour – that means it is very good. I am very good at drawing. Everybody likes my pictures and I won the competition to do the picture and it was judged the best in the whole world by children. My drawing was a picture of the pry mintser. It was called Portrait. And he's smiling and got big eyes and he's everso nice and I did my picture just like that. Everybody said, 'It's amazing and incredible and unbelievable and him just a kid. It's a special talent he's got,' everybody says.

And because I won, the pry mintser will come to our school while he is in the town doing something else as well. He will see me and shake hands and it is an honour because they say, 'Your picture is the winner and it is so perfect like him.'

* *

It was exciting. I saw him coming. He needed two cars. 'That's because he's so important, and has lots of baggage,' my friend William said.

And two people with him had guns. 'I bet that's to make him behave himself,' Mary Atkins said. 'My mum waves a stick at me.'

We had the assembly with all the school there, and there was all the talking and clapping and they gave me my prize. And there were some people with cameras there and they made like a film of it.

153

When we came off the stage I said, 'He didn't shake my hand and that was supposed to be the big honour.' So I followed him when he came down. And I went up to him with my hand out for him to shake and I said, 'You didn't get the honour, so here I am.'

But he just looked at me. And he looked at my hand. And he had a funny look. And he didn't want to shake my hand. So I said, 'It's your honour and you deserve it.' But he didn't want to. He didn't say so, but the way he looked at my hand. Well, I left it there sticking out at him and I smiled more. And he looked and his smile wasn't there. He looked at my hand like it was dirty. It wasn't. 'It's clean,' I told him. 'I licked it clean again, like I did when I went on stage and wiped it on my shirt.' There was a bit of chocolate down the back of it, but not enough to bother about. I licked most of it off, anyway, before I reached out to him.

His face was gone all like froze and not liking me. I don't know what he was thinking, but he didn't have any smile in him at all. His eyes went pointy like little finger holes and his nose twitched. Then he went away.

I looked at my hand where I still had it sticking out for him. 'I don't think he wanted the honour after all,' I told William.

We looked at my hand again. 'It looks alright to me,' William said, and licked the big smudge of chocolate off.

* *

So I did another picture of him with his not-smiling face – looking all beady and cross. My teacher said, 'That's very good and very different and did he really look like that?'

And I said, 'Yes.'

The lady with the man with the camera came back the next day and talked with my teacher and then talked with me, and they took another photograph of me with my new picture and they said, 'Can you look sad instead of happy?'

* *

There was eversuch a lot of fuss about it. Some people said my number two picture was exactly like he actually was. And it was on the television and the front page of a newspaper – it was my picture of him and they said he had showed how nasty he was really.

Somebody wants him to be not pry mintser anymore because he didn't want the honour to shake my hand. The newspaper man said, 'This just shows him like he really is.'

'It speaks voll yumes,' the lady on the television said. But the pry mintser didn't speak to me at all.

My mum says, 'I bet he wishes he did now. They really want him to be not pry mintser anymore.'

DWINDLING

We started proud and we started green
On Omaha Beach baptised in fire.
To get through the waves was hell for most.
Brothers and sons stained golden sand with crimson blood.
Though we're not as many as we used to be,
We're confident yet: the 44th'll be going home.
But our numbers now are dwindling low.

Eight-foot hedgehogs and tangled wire
Trapped us there, while the guns took toll
And mowed us down like a field of wheat.
Not many survived to scale that cliff.
Familiar faces are dwindling still.
We left good men on Omaha Beach.

We engaged them hard to the Falaise Gap.
In eleven days of hammering shot and blazing shell
We took out the panzers with our M5 guns.
But it *didn't* come cheap, like the general said.
So many died, and our roll call's dwindling yet.

Surrounded then in Bastogne town
In bitter cold, ten bullets each and nothing to eat.
Surrender, demanded the Jerry foe. Our general sneered.
Nuts, he said, and we fought on, we dwindling few.

To the Rhine at Remagen we battled and died.
Dwindling still, we crossed that bridge to the Fatherland.
But we were a platoon at most who reached Cologne.

I'm the only one left of the 44th; and I'm dwindling, too:
In Manchester I lost my legs to a concert bomb

And a devil called Hate that stalks the land.

STEFFF

'Steffff?'

'*Stephanie,*' I told him. 'My name's *Stephanie.* Get it right, Stanley.' I pressed the red key, and put the phone down. My younger half-brother always insists on calling me that, purely to irritate me. Mum had named me Stephanie, had me christened Stephanie Sylvia, and always used my full name. When will that dozy dropout learn? It's only marginally less annoying than what my older brother calls me sometimes: 'Fanny.' He means it in a derogatory way, every time he says it. He still says it now we're all so-called adults.

'Okay, I got better things to do than answer the phone to a wally half-brother intent on chalking me off.' I turned back to The American Journal of Medicine. This month's is especially interesting: particularly the parts about me. The personal profile is the standard one page insight and ego-booster that I'd worked on with the journalist who visited one day. The inset photo at the top is the rather nice one of me from the front cover of my "art" portfolio. *Mmm, yes, I do look good.* As the secondary headline said, "Smart in Every Way". They've placed my profile immediately following my research report on arterial bypass techniques, directions and practicalities. It had been *so* well received in two international symposia, receiving plaudits from absolutely everywhere. It's to be reprinted in the BMJ next month. They'll be carrying this profile, too.

Quite pleasing, really.

Stanley. My useless younger brother. A so-called artist, specialising in smirking, taking the mick, cadging cash, and rarely producing anything – whether of note or not. At least we aren't fully related: Mum married again after my father died of something heart-related. They never said what. It was what got me into cardiology. Stanley is, thankfully, only my half-brother. For around half-a-second I wondered what he'd rung for. He could text or email like normal people, couldn't he? Not that he ever bothered, unless he was scrounging for another free vacation in California. *He's not bringing his awful brood over here to stay with me again.*

Ahh… ringing my international tone, 'Bugger, it's him again. He can talk to the answerphone.' On the eighth ring, I relented, 'Sod you,' I cussed, touched the answer button, and waited.

'For sod's sake, *Stephanie Sylvia,* just bloody listen will you?' Yes, that's Stanley's dulcet tone, alright. 'Stuart had an accident yesterday – don't know what happened. Something on this city-centre job, you know?'

'No, I don't know.'

'Well, he's bad; injured. You need to come.'

'Why? Is he not likely to survive?' I could feel a growing cold lump in my chest.

'They won't say – operating today. You should come, Steff… anie. He is your bloody brother, remember.'

'Okay… okay… okay.' I took all the details… consultant… hospital… ward. 'I'll be there soon as. How are you?' But there wasn't an answer – the phone went dead. He was probably saving pennies.

'Shit.' I *have* to go: 'He *is* my older brother.' I suppose Stuart had done well; he made a good living as an "abstract architect" who was always keen to be on site, interfering. Some big projects were his, in London, Paris,

Adelaide, wherever else. I'd never have thought it of Stuart. Not that we had anything to do with each other these days. His three brats were spoiled, ill-behaved, and had virtually wrecked the guest apartment at my house. So I avoid them when I'm back in the UK.

But, family is family. I cancelled the lecture I was to give, off-loaded four operations, cried out of the evening party, and booked a flight back to UK. First class was the only seat they had. 'What!!! How much?' My caterwauling didn't help – they stuck to the extortionate price; and introduced a special-off six-hour transfer in Atlanta. 'It's the only way to get you there.'

'*Atlanta?* That airport is populated by the most obnoxious security staff I ever came across anywhere, including Tambo, Jo'berg. Can't I have a twelve-hour delay in JFK? Ohh… alright.' So I got my money's worth of everything from arse-licking to buckets of Bollinger. It crossed my mind that it might look as if I were celebrating; *but who cares what anyone thinks?*

I surprised myself. I actually worried about him. Older brother? Not seen each other for a couple of years. We got on well enough as children, I suppose. Sometimes. Nothing deep and bonding. He bullied me sometimes, looked after me sometimes.

'It's what brothers do,' he kicked me when I was beating him at ice skating. I've still got the scar on my calf to prove it. Ice skates'll do that.

'It's what brothers do,' when he tackled some creep who was all over me one night. Gave him a right ball-bruising, he did. Good with his feet like that, was Stuart.

Then some bloody taxi bastard ripped me off getting from the airport to the hospital. But it was midnight, and they weren't letting anyone in. Even *me!* Not unless the patient was actually dying. They checked: he wasn't on the pre-mort list. 'So *bugger off*,' was the look on the little turd's face. Security arrived and pushed me towards the taxi rank. Talk about a foul mood and a hangover – I had both.

'Why I put myself through all this is quite beyond me, especially after the way he laughed about his brats setting fire to their beds in the apartment – then flooding it when it suddenly spread.'

'No, they are not just doing what kids will do,' I told him.

'Just because yours don't. Fucking little saints, huh?'

'Eight thousand dollars,' I told the taxi driver. I could have told him anything – he didn't speak any English except a few place names. 'Stuart was the one who walked in on me in the shower – three times!' I saw the driver glance in the mirror then, so maybe he did speak some English. 'It was Stuart who ripped up my essay about the blight of modern architecture – it would have won the Sixth Form Prize. But a few weeks later he took a day off to drive me up to Manchester for an interview. We loaned each other money or paid for things, and never even thought about asking for it back. He always called me a titless wonder… but I saw him one night when we were partying, trying to get his mate to pick me up. He was saying, 'No, she's okay, actually.' High praise indeed from him.

So I rang the ward first thing next morning, after a foul and very expensive night in some filthy modern hotel, probably one that Stuart designed. They downright refused to tell me anything. 'Are you close family?'

'Yes, sister.'

But they didn't believe me, 'There's been no mention of a sister on his details,' and the phone went dead.

'Hardly surprising the NHS is in a mess,' I swore at the phone. 'No wonder I pushed off, soon as.'

I rang back. 'Open visiting is not permitted. Unless a patient is dying. He's not on the critical list. You're not next of kin.'

'Yes, I bloody am,' I said to the buzzing phone. 'For God's sake, is he bloody worth it? I might as well have stayed in Cali-fucking-fornia.

'Okay okay okay. Calm yourself.' I ate some breakfast, even if it was nine at night, Pacific Time. To be honest, a full English is something the Americans just can't do. They miss out on the burned sausage, the discoloured tomatoes, the blackened bacon, the crust on the lump of baked beans, the swills of grease, the brown sauce, the black pudding, and *real* hash browns. So it put me in a better mood, until the acid indigestion set it. I deserved it – I'd worked for it.

Normal visiting was at two in the afternoon, so I conferenced on a couple of my operations back home in California: they'd managed just great without me. That is really good to know: my teaching's been worthwhile.

'We can't have too many people at the bedside,' the gruesome little porter told me. A porter, for God's sake! Not even a nurse. Pulling rank got me nowhere. I mean, I *am* a senior doctor, an Attending, for God's sake. I had my initial training in this bloody hospital, even if I never worked here afterwards.

So eventually, I joined in with all the other visitors wandering worriedly along the corridor towards HD6, the High Dependency ward where he was supposed to be. But, of course he wasn't there. 'He's not out of Intensive Care yet,' Some haggard nurse with an actinic keratosis on her nose told me. 'We'll let you know if you wait, over *there*. And No, you can't go to Intensive Care – they

163

don't allow more than two people at a time in there, if any.' Frosty-faced cow.

'You should get that seen to,' I pointed at her nose.

She gave me the extra-frigid look, 'Wait. *There*. We'll tell you. Don't try to get in again.' Stone-faced 10-year-old masquerading as a 28-year-old imbecile. Or vice versa.

It was the same with all of them. *Screw me backwards. There are better things to do with my time. If that bugger isn't at least headless, armless and legless, I'm going to be really chalked off.* It was ridiculous. I was fuming. Where were all the others, anyway? Stanley? Stuart's wife – Genevieve and those revolting kids – Aubyn, Barclay and Annabelle? It made me sick to mentally pronounce their names.

And Stanley's brood – partner Maisie, and urchins Jack, Jim, Jo, Joe, Jessie, Jesse, and, as I recall, Jemeldina. At least we aren't *fully* related. I like to dismiss them as merely related by marriage, only half by blood.

'Here comes the SS.' He used to call me that when we were little and I tried to get him to behave; Stephanie Sylvia, hmm.

'What the hell are *you* doing here?' I froze. I know that appalling voice. Stanley, coming up behind me.

'What are you doing *here?*' said Maisie, little and fat.

'Took yer time, didn't ya?'

'Is that Aunty Steffeee?' Little git – he spent a fortnight at my place last summer. My samoyeds still haven't recovered.

Appalling toads. I squashed them with a dead stare, bursting in here like an avalanche of sheep. Stanley standing there, blonde hair that straggled worse than a thousand spiders on methamphetamine. Never done a day's work in his life. Maisie worked as a cleaner somewhere, on nights, last I heard. *I bet you shrivel up in the sunlight.*

Stuart's wife came in, Genevieve. We nodded and half-smiled. She was an even snottier bitch than I am. She's never once, ever, asked about my two, or how I'd been after the miscarriage, or the op. Not once. But nor had any of the others, either. I don't know why I bother.

Talk about stilted conversations. I really, *really* wished I'd stayed home. I could have conferenced through, zoomed, or something, not spent two days getting here, missing my kids. *God! – all the commitments I dropped out of, for this pathetic ignorant lot.* Despair wasn't the half of it.

Family is family. I'm not here for them. Okay, so they despise me. It's mutual. 'Very well,' I said, 'if you can cease sneering at me from your gutter, how's Stuart?'

I might as well have talked to the Walking Dead for all they reacted. *Ghouls,* I thought. *Blank-faced. Open-mouthed.*

'Yeah, for all you care, Stefffff.' He'd always been a little toe-rag, Stanley. I merely shot him another hate-look.

I'm here for Stuart, nobody else, I insisted to myself. 'Okay, whether I care or not, how is he? Is he still all there? Not that he ever was before.'

Stanley had this sneaky laugh; I always thought he practised it for when he was being devious. 'We saw him yesterday while you were swanning round in the sun.' His eyes flicked behind me, 'They're bringing him in from Intensive Care. Go see for yourself, seeing as you've taken your time sauntering over here.'

'While we've been here for him all the time.'

They want me to be pissed off for coming, when he's okay all along. Having their laugh. Or, if Stuart is bad, for me to say something spiteful, and show myself up.

He's going to be fine, I decided; *he'd still be in ICU if he was critical.*

'I'll come with you,' Stanley volunteered. 'He'll recognise *me*.'

'Asshole,' I told him as we went in. 'You've always been a half-baked pillock, Stanley. As well as a half-baked brother.'

Stuart was just being wheeled in, his bed being spun round and pushed against the wall; plugging him into a dozen monitors and drips. The nurses eventually dissipated as we waited there.

Sitting up, Stuart saw me. Face scowled. 'What you doing here?' He scowled at Stanley, 'What d'y bring *her* for?'

Even sitting up in bed, I could see he was shorter. Two feet shorter. Two calves gone as well, with the tib and fib. And the knees. And half his thighs as well. He looked ridiculous. A single sheet draped itself across him. It flopped to bed level six inches below his groin.

His legs have gone.

It was a shock, sure enough. Nothing I could say. He was staring at me, so sodding sour, the miserable toad. Well, he needn't bloody bother, making me feel guilty, wallowing in being miserable. It wasn't me who collapsed his stupid half-built building all over him and smashed his legs up.

'Huh,' I sneered at him, 'you should have had the day *I've* had – it started sixty hours ago, while you sit there in bed, you selfish git, and drag me all the way over here.'

That shocked him. I bet the others had all been silent sympathy shrouds round him. But he and I never minced

166

anything. I stomped over to him. I could feel tears going to burst out and I wasn't going to do that for *anybody*.

'You do *this* to me?' I was furious. I bent and smacked his face, hard. God that surprised him. Me, too. 'Now I only have *one* brother.'

'Eh?' That shook him just as much.

'Stan's my half-brother. Now there's only half of *you*. That leaves me with only one whole one.'

God alone knows how I dared to say it. But I had. There was silence. Talk about gob-smacked. The women and kids behind me, corporate breath held. A pair of narky nurses were recovering first, starting towards me. He was touching his cheek. It must have really hurt, I'd caught him just right. *He deserves it for doing this to me.*

'Sod me, Sis. Trust you.' His face was splitting into a rueful grin. Big laugh, 'No pussyfooting with you, eh?' He grabbed at me, pulling me next to him. He squawked as I landed half on his stumps. But he was laughing, 'This lot haven't dared say a word. I've been too grumpy. Thank God for a bit of normality. Come here…'

He was hugging me, and laughing. 'Back like when we were kids, eh?'

I know my eyes were brimming up. 'Yeah, right,' I was saying, laughing through the tears. 'I remember the last time, when I was twelve. But *this* time,' I prodded at his residual limbs. Both amputated halfway down the *rectus femorus* muscle, 'you *can't* put me over your knees and spank me now, can you?'

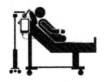

DOCTOR JOHNSON

Judge Jeffreys was arrogant. He would call people by their title if he felt like it, or if he thought they were on the same side – Inspector, Constable, Reverend, but not the witness of an accident, whom he took a dislike to and suspected might not be truthful about his evidence.

'You're merely a witness, not giving expert evidence in your field of qualification. A doctor of mathematics, you say? That's irrelevant. In here, you're *Mister* – if that. Just another public witness.'

'But it is my title, like Albert Einstein, and I'm, er, entitled to be called by it, Your Honour.' Dr Johnson politely replied.

'In my court, you're *mister.*'

'Okay, Mr Jeffreys, we'll settle on that then.'

'You call me, "Judge Jeffreys, Your Honour!"'

Sam shook his head, 'That's a lot of title. How long have you had it?'

'Eight years, and I—''

'Well, I've been a doctor since 1989. That's a lot longer. So I've got precedent over you, George. I've got certificates and photographs to prove it.'

'One more peep from you, Johnson, and I'll have you charged with contempt of court. Do you understand?' He was quite enraged.

'Yes,' Sam shrugged, '*George.*'

His Honour, Judge George Jeffreys, was incandescent, but moderately controlled, 'The officer of the court will take Mister Johnson to the cells to consider his attitude.'

Sam held the officer at bay, 'He said to take *Mister* Johnson down. That's not me. I'm *Doctor* Johnson. And that's more of a doctorate than my predecessor had. You know, Doctor Samuel Johnson, Eighteenth Century? His doctorate was only honorary – never had to work for it like I did.'

The Officer of the Court wasn't having any of that, and nodded to the two security men at the back.

Sam had more sense than to resist, but he wasn't cooperating, either, and allowed himself to be carried unresistingly down three flights of head-banging stairs to the cells.

An hour changed his mind not one jot. 'After two-dozen or so fracturing bumps to my skull, I can't see out my right eye; my specs have gone; I got a stinking headache; my elbow's swelled up stiff as a board, and that pillock wants me up there to apologise? He can whistle for it. Tell him I need a doctor first.'

The message from the courtroom was back within minutes, 'You're the doctor: Heal thyself, physician.'

The court messenger was almost apologetic, 'Also, Doctor Johnson, the defendant in the case has been taken ill; a doctor was called, and the defendant is being escorted to hospital. You're to be remanded in custody until the court session resumes – tomorrow.'

Ninety minutes later, in the company of three other prisoners, Dr Sam Johnson found himself standing in the bare reception room of the remand wing at Northington Prison. Two guards checked the prisoner-batch over, made them strip, and gave out grey remand onesies.

'Smith?'

'Yessir,' one stepped forward.

'You're Prisoner 4912,'

'Yessir.'

'It's like the army,' Johnson marvelled, as Smith was allowed to don his onesie with his new prison number scrawled in felt-tip on the chest patch.

The others, the same. Numbered, dressed, stood in a row.

Then it was his turn. 'Johnson.' He was pushed forward.

'*Doctor* Johnson,' he corrected politely, peering blurredly out of his damaged eye. 'I'm entitled to my title.'

'Not in here. In here, you're 4915.'

'I think you'll find that's *Prisoner* 4915… *Ufff!!!*' as the guard's baton slammed into the back of his knee.

'I see. We're going to have trouble with *you*, are we?'

Alone in his hospital room, Dr Johnson attempted to sit up, but his legs were fixed in the network of wires and pulleys, and the half-acre of plastered bandages that swathed both legs, his ribs and newly-shaven skull. His back was already strapped and tensioned, and would remain so for another four weeks.

'You've caused enough bother and delay, you have. Provoking the prison staff in that manner.' The three police officers and two technical assistants were wise, and had decided not to put his back up again by refusing to call him Doctor. So they simply didn't use any form of address.

'If you're speaking to him,' Sergeant Randolph had briefed them, 'look directly at him, make eye contact. A fingertip touch at most, to ensure his attention. We need his testimony for the case against the Della Street gang. The time runs out tomorrow. Lick his arse and kiss his dick if you must. Get. That. Testimony.'

171

Dr Johnson hadn't relented in his obduracy about how he should be formally addressed on such an occasion. Equally, he wasn't feeling too good, especially as "his" nurse insisted on calling him "Sammy-Luv", and "forgetting" to actually administer the dihydromorphine that she removed from the drugs cabinet four times a day in his name. 'And you can forget about me calling you "Doctor", Sammy-Luv. The only doctors in here got white coats and stethoscopes. So you can whistle for your meds, hmm? Oh, you can't whistle, can you? Without your front teeth.'

'Alright then, Doctor Johnson—' the sergeant forgot himself and accidentally used the preferred form of address. 'Well,' he apologised, 'my father was a Ph.D. and everybody called him "Doctor" the same and we liked that and he was entitled. So, *Dr* Johnson, are we ready to proceed? We have the witnesses for your statement, here...' they nodded and mumbled something with "doctor" in it. 'And my colleagues manning the video and audio-recording equipment.' They all nodded politely, 'Doctor... constable. Hi, doctor... morning...'

'Right,' the sergeant said, mightily relieved to have all this idiotic silliness over, 'To continue, you are still under oath, as though in the witness box in court, that unfortunate day. You understand, Doctor Johnson?'

Samuel nodded, 'I do,' feeling as though he were getting married again – he'd felt rough that day, too, after the glorious stag night from hell. 'Let's get on, shall we?'

They all thought they understood his tooth-bereft, jaw-wired words, and everyone relaxed, the equipment running sweetly and silently. 'You are Doctor Samuel Johnson? State your name and date of birth, please.' The sergeant listened carefully, translated the mumbles to English, confirmed his interpretation with a nod from

172

Samuel, and re-checked his notes, and nodded all round, receiving a nod back from the technicians – the equipment was recording correctly. *Thank God for that.* He settled to his case notes and the list of questions of all the points that needed to be verified if the case against the Della Street gang was to be pursued successfully on the morrow.

Big smile, 'and can you confirm that you were proceeding along Bole Street 8.30 p.m. on the 22nd August last, when the accused pair ran across the busy road and, unprovoked, attacked the old lady? Can you tell us in your own words what then occurred?'

'No.'

'Eh?' Alarm bells jangled all through Sergeant Randolph's body. *What the hell is it this time?* He controlled himself, sorely tempted to finish the job the prison guards had begun on the stubborn cretin in the bed. He eyed up the tubes and switches – so easy to accidentally trip over something, knock a switch... This case was vital. His evidence *must* be obtained today. Feeling a little empty, 'You can't? Or you won't?'

'It wasn't me.' The words were gluggling in Samuel's throat, but were understood, juts the same. 'It was the other Doctor Sam Johnson.'

'The other one?' Four voices echoed.

Samuel tried to nod, but the strapping didn't permit such movements. 'Doctor *Samantha* Johnson. My wife. Nobody'd listen to us.'

'Okay, okay.' This was still salvageable. 'Where may we find her?'

'She's in the next war—'

'Come on!' Sergeant Randolph cut him short. 'Next ward. Get this lot packed up. Quick.'

173

Out he dashed to lead the way, down between the rows of beds, slamming to a halt at the barred double doors and plastic sheeting at the far end of the ward. The red-on-yellow sign could hardly be missed, "Covid ICU. Coma Unit. No Entry".

He stood in silence for long, long moments, imagining the good doctor to be lying, comatose, deep into pressurised oxygen, or whatever they did with their severe Covid victims. 'Our case is dead; they'll get away with it... we're out of time.' Slowly, deliberately, he began to tear up his case notes, page by page. Wiping the tears from his eyes, he turned to face the ward, and trudge back past Samuel's side-room.

'Oo ee urr?' Samuel said something as he passed

'What?' He went in, 'What did you say?'

'Id oo see her? She's off doo-ee in ten minutes.'

'Off duty? Off duty?' Slowly backing out, 'You mean she's not dying and isolated and incubating in there?. Sergeant Randolph gazed down the length of the ward, between the beds, where an auxiliary nurse was sweeping up his widely scattered mass of shredded notes.

'Shit,' he said.

THE PLOT AGAINST
KING AETHELWULF

Let it be known in this second year of the reign of King Aethelwulf of West Mercia, the year as reckoned by the Romanic calendar as 765. This the decree of the Hundred of Amwythig, under the power granted by the Witan of King Aethelwulf. Be it known that the trial of the pretender Dyhlithbec has taken place in the Great Hall at Amwythig.

The execution of Dyhli Dyhlithbec and his Lawful-by-Church Wife, the Lady Seaxburth shall take place at the High Crossroads by Shrewksbury Bridge on the fourth day of Eostremonath at evenset. The execution shall be by hanging by the neck.

It is declared that, in full accordance with the law of the land, and of the lords, the council of the Hundred of Wythig considered the testimony of many witnesses and former supporters of the insurrectional pair. Letters and other documents showing clear guilt were submitted, and were fully and publicly examined. Account was also given of numerous false tales, rumours and rebel songs spread among the people of West Mercia by the close advisors and other perpetrators of this plot to overthrow King Aethelwulf.

The Hundred has affirmed the rightful place of kingship of King Aethelwulf and Queen Arianrod; and in so doing has thereby rejected the case put to the people by Dyhlithbec and Lady Seaxburth. The denials by both persons were finally dismissed when three witnesses to the Lady Seaxburth's frequent singing of the deceivers'

Battle Song came forward in a grant of amnesty under law.

The spreading of usurper rumours, and the singing of seditious songs will henceforth be punishable by the cutting out of the tongue. In the aforesaid Battle Song, there is clear calling for the uprising to begin when the lavender is in full bloom, in the monath of Liða. This fact is linked unfailingly to the lines, 'When the lavender's bloom, Dyhli Dyhli; when lavender's green; you will be King, Dyhli Dyhlithbec, and I'll be your Queen.'

THE PRAM LADY

A woman was wheeling an old pram along the opposite pavement. Stupid, being out on a dark cold night like this. 'You ought to be rolled up in your cardboard,' I was thinking, 'Not pushing a pram full of blankets and trash collectings round the streets.' She was continually bending and tucking the rain cover back down when the wind lifted it up, flapping it around. The wind was picking up; *You'll be even busier with that cover if you don't stop and button it down securely.* She clutched her long coat to her chest.

Idly, I watched her on her intermittent way, stopping to adjust the cover or kick one of the rear wheels back onto its axle. Probably a pram she'd pulled out the canal and filled with her stinking raggy clothes and a hundred filthy newspapers.

I watched her in total disinterest. *I got plenty enough troubles of my own. February 14th, and I'm alone.* The wonderful evening I had planned for the two of us was gone with the wind and the flurries of sleet. Jennifer had turned me down – my proposal and the evening at Sir Vesa's – my favourite Mexican restaurant and show. I often went there, and was known to the staff, so I was usually successful in asking for a side table near the stage. What a great evening it would have been.

But tonight, Jennifer had turned me down, and added a few choice comments to see me on my way: she decided to enlighten me with a few home truths, as she called her spiteful vindictiveness. 'You're greedy and selfish; you never give a thought to other people.'

'Why should I?' I'd asked, 'no-one thinks of me.'

177

'I do,' she said, 'or I did. But I've had enough.' She stared at the ring I'd bought in distaste. 'Marriage to you would be the stuff of nightmares. You have no love of life, no charity… "The greatest of these is Charity,"' she quoted, 'remember your bible?'

'Mistranslation,' I told her. 'It should have been Faith, Hope and *Love*.'

'You're also pedantic.'

'I prefer to get things right, not be fobbed off with half-truths and jobs half-done,' I informed her in return.

Just the same, Jennifer had gone. Out the apartment, and out of my life. 'Forever,' she insisted when I'd laughed, 'You'll be back soon enough. Where will you sleep?'

'At Matlock's – Colin Matlock; he's asked me out many times, including today. I said I would give him my answer this evening.'

'*Him?* He's a thicko. He can barely string two words together; pathetic job, a wage about a tenth of mine.' It was to no avail.

'You're tight-fisted you're snobby and you have no empathy for anyone.' She put a lot of feeling into saying that as she made a couple of calls and began clearing her few things out. It didn't take her long.

When she'd gone, I walked out, and wandered alone. The evening had darkened up quickly, both in my mood and the cold city streets.

Sudden squall; I'd come into this dingy little café diner, ordered a hot chocolate and took a shabby seat by the window. 'And your favourite saying,' she told me, 'is so demeaning, "Wonder what the poor people are doing?" every time you throw money away on an extravagant trip or meal,'

178

'Yes, well, so what? They're poor because they're stupid and/or won't work – they should have paid attention in school.'

The old pram woman was returning down this side of the street, the wind and sleet at her back now. Her black hat had gone and her hair was lifting past her face, hiding her features. I imagined them to be gaunt and determined. As such people need to be.

'You feel nothing for anyone. You're not normal.'

'It's normal for me,' I told her. Jenny was right there – I have no empathy for others and their situations. Why should I? 'People get themselves into their own messes: they should get themselves out. I never go cringing for help anywhere.'

Like this woman: the wheel had finally come off her pram and she was backing into the sheltered doorway of the diner, bending down to fix it, then kneeling in the darkness. I wouldn't have bothered to watch her, but there was nothing else to look at in there, and the street was deserted.

My hot chocolate was warming – a bit too warming – the milk had been boiled and it burned my lip. I cursed it, almost laughing that my mood couldn't become much worse if anything else went wrong. So I cheered myself up watching the stupid bloody woman fiddling with the pram wheel in the doorway. Someone was wanting to get past her, pushing at her and the pram to get out of his way. She wasn't much good at making me feel any better. It was a large man with a lumberjack coat and an overly energetic dog with muzzle and chain. Pushing the door open, he was cursing her, telling her to get out the way. He came in with an arrogant grin. Not that he had anything to be arrogant about – overweight and unsightly, with cuffs frayed on his jacket.

179

Pram woman hadn't gone. 'Good for you,' I smiled. She must be accustomed to such treatment and let it wash over her. Yes, well, we all have our troubles – like the fat, ugly feller with a dog to match; and the diner girl with the awful pink-chequered uniform and worse accent; me with a tender lip and half a mile to walk back home while the sleet was settling in.

Watching another squally gust blow through, I decided to go. 'I better get it over with.' Calling the girl over, I paid for the chocolate, and told her it had been too hot, but left a decent tip anyway.

'You always tip well,' Jenny once told me, 'It massages your ego.'

The bloody woman was still there with her crippled pram when I arrived at the door and pulled it open. 'Kick that bitch out the way,' a voice shouted behind me. 'Or I'll send Nitro to see you both out.'

'Will you indeed?' I muttered and turned to look at the Fat Ugly pair. I was in no mood for being threatened by a redneck toe-rag like him. So I bent down to see if I could help her, purely to piss him off. *Nobody* tells me what to do. She was struggling with the wheel – it needed a bent pin through the hole in the axle, and it was missing.

'The big guy says he'll turn the dog on you if you don't shut the door and clear off.' The girl with the accent had come to relay the message.

'Okay,' I told her. 'Come on, you.' I pulled the woman up and started backing into the diner with her and the pram. Brooking no protest from her or the pink-chequered girl, I dragged the reluctant pram and woman back to my seat in the window. I knelt next to the pram, 'Let's see what we can do with this. You sit there. You want a drink? Something to eat?' I slapped a twenty on the table. 'Call Pinky over – have whatever you want.'

She didn't move. I looked up from the axle bar. That was a shock – she was young, not the old bag I'd imagined. A soft face, smooth. I'd expected her to be drawn and pinched with hard eyes. But hers were a soft brown.

That threw me entirely. Fat Ugly called something from across the room again. It sounded ominous. 'Order something,' I told Prammy. 'I'll have the same, whatever. Something that's slow to eat. *Sit.*' Head down, I was back attending to the wheel – the tine of a fork would probably jam into the hole and bend double to keep the wheel in place.

A scratching, snuffling sound from the depths of the pram took my attention. 'Hello,' I thought, 'You're on the street and you've got a flea-bitten terrier as well.' The weather cover moved. I lifted it and looked. There were two of the tiny things in there, both dark-eyed little monstrosities that stared malevolently up at me, eyes glittering, blaming. 'You've got twin babies in here.' Okay, so it was a stupid thing to say, but I was more than a mite surprised. *Besides, you shouldn't be whoring round and getting yourself with child; it's worse than having a dog.*

But, it was nothing to do with me… and Fat Ugly was demanding something, standing up now, looking our way. I was still kneeling between the table and her pram, 'Pass me the tray,' I told her, 'with the spare cutlery rolls, napkins and condiments.' I fiddled with a fork for a moment, did a temporary fix on the wheel, and used a couple of napkins to wipe the rust and grease off my hands. 'I thought you'd have your bedding in there.'

I sat opposite her and pulled the pram closer, just as Fat Ugly turned up with dog on chain, but its muzzle was off, and it was straining to get at us. Teeth dribbling and

181

drooling, red-eyed and raving – and the dog was just as bad. But, he'd given us plenty of notice of his intentions, and I'm not one to ignore warnings. The top was off the pepper pot, and the chilli-dip bowl was handy.

The dog took a faceful of wet chilli, and Fat Ugly Feller was screaming with the pepper in his eyes and mouth. The shrieking and ranting! The dog was instantly howling and clawing and pawing and rounding on its master, though neither could see a thing. He was trying to paw at his face, but the chain was round his wrist. He was roaring and cursing.

'Shall we go? It's getting rowdy in here.' Dumbly, she nodded, and we squeezed out the seats and trundled her pram out.

'You didn't get your drink… or anything to eat… Do you know anywhere else round here?'

She didn't. I walked alongside her. 'Are the babies alright?'

'I need to feed them.'

'How?'

'Either… There's powder in the pram basket, but I need to warm some water. Or feed them myself if there's somewhere that allows it.'

'How come you're out here, like this?' The look she gave me… I backed off. 'Sorry. I'm not really nosy.'

So we walked in silence, except one of the twins started off. 'My partner… boyfriend… threw me out. We had a row. He's been seeing someone else. He said I was always thinking of the babies, and never of him. So he told me I should clear off and spend as long as I wanted thinking about the damned selfish creatures. That was… a couple of hours ago.'

About the same time Jennifer was throwing herself out of my place. 'There's a pizza place across the road.'

It was packed – some show had just turned out. There was a queue forty deep. Buggerit. The wimpy kid in the pram was starting to cry. Buggerit again. The queue wasn't moving – people had huge take-out orders, as well as the crowded tables inside…

'What's your name?'

She looked reluctant to say, 'Why?' Then she relented, 'Adina. My girls are Rachel and Miriam.'

'Something occurs to me, Adina, I live not far from here – maybe twenty minutes by pram. Perhaps, if you want, you could come, and I could warm something up?' The look on her face! You'd think I just smacked her.

'Leave me alone – I don't need your charity. Go away. I don't need you.' She meant it. She still had the twenty I'd put on the table in the diner. 'I don't need you.'

'Okay. If that's your attitude, you can get stuffed.' *Again.* I turned to go, even more chalked off than when the evening began. But this was different now. I was pissed off because… because… why? Because she hadn't let me help her? Where the hell do I get off? Almost helping somebody? That is not me. But – once in a lifetime, I do offer – and I get told to piss off. Yeah, right. That's the last time. Ever. That I try to help anybody. Ungrateful cow.

So now I got my empty apartment to look forward to. No Jennifer. Ah, shugger… I'll have to stick something on the grill. Full English, maybe. See what's on Netflix. Must remember to turn the heating up when I walk in. Damn moronic woman. Her two brats are probably just as dim-witted.

Whoa – the wind was picking up. Blustering more. I turned. Still at the Pizza dump. Looking in like she was going to outwait the queue – fat chance – it was already longer, and she'd never get that useless pram in there.

183

Shrugged. Nothing to do with me. I don't do caring. I often told myself that. Yeah, Jennifer told me, too, 'You just couldn't care less, could you?'

'Nope,' I'd say, and put on my smug smirk. *I'll have to do my own bangers and eggs tonight, though.*

Like Jenny said on the way out tonight, 'You're a shit, Timothy. A selfish shit.'

Lordy, that sleet's slushing up round my feet. Shoes'll get wet, spoil the leather. So what? Vicious blast whipping my collar up. Pram-brain clutching at the hood as it jerked about in the wind. Glad I'm not—

I stopped to do up the top button more securely. She was still last in the queue. Wouldn't want to be…

Looked back when another gust rocked me. Still there. So useless. How stupid is she? I can't imagine what…

How'd anybody let themselves get in that state? Huh, like I care?

Do I?

Do I care?

She turned as I touched her shoulder. Damp-eyed, but harder now. Jaw set. 'I told you: I don't need you.'

'Maybe you don't need me… but… I think I need you.'

THE TEN COMMAND MOMENTS

"The Ecumenical Conference of All Higher Thought" was the endeavourant name given to the beautiful aspiration of having three days of exchange, reason and discussion among and between representatives of several major religions, and various atheist and secular groups. The hope was magnificent. The date was carefully chosen – early May, when there was the National Day of Prayer, which enveloped half the delegates, and the Day of Reason, which satisfied the other half. The expectations weren't high: to have some exchange of views in a rational manner, in a calm setting – "a Beginning of Sharing" agreed the joint organisers.

'A beginning will be sufficient of an aim for our first great meeting,' sagely nodded the elders on one side, and the Asails on the other side. Asails? Atheists, skeptics, agnostics, infidels and libertines. They rather liked their acronym.

'Looking at the lists of attendees,' opined Ms Dzika Karta, 'There may be reluctance to begin the discussions, to express oneself, to be open and free…'

'We don't want reticence…'

'Or unheeding dogma.'

'Perhaps a Keynote Speaker to set an open tone on the morning of the first Thursday in May…'

'To free up some willingness to speak…'

'I may know of someone…?' tentatively offered Mr Vrije Denker.

Impatient to have the matter settled, it was left in the
hands of Vrije, the well-known Free Thinker from
Holland, Michigan.

Come the first Thursday morning of May, there was a
definite air of hope in the Great Hall of The People,
Kansas City – the largest available hall that was close to
the geographic centre of the country, "and therefore close
to its heart,' it was commonly said.

To polite, expectant applause, Signore Merda Agitatoré
ascended the seven steps to the stage and took his place
at the lectern. Bowing slightly to left, right and centre, he
spoke in a delicate Italian accent, without using notes or
tele-prompter. 'Ladies and Gentlemen, I shall speak for
around ten minutes, in a series of ten points. I think of
them as the Ten Command Moments of Religion. Then
you will be free to ask questions, or to raise any topics
that you may wish to discuss amongst yourselves.
'You are all seated comfortably?'

1   Adam and Eve? Well. They were on a loser from
the off – You should have heard'em.

They reckoned they'd heard a snake talking
to'em. What were they on then? I'll tell you what – it
was the apples. Don't eat the apples, the snake said, so,
naturally, they don't. I mean – you do what snakes tell
you, huh? Eve, of course, being Eve, said, 'You know
what you can do with your apples, don't you, Ad-lad?

'Make cider,' he says. 'The chatty snake only said
don't *eat* them, nothing about drinking them.'

The bother arose when they forgot that cider ferments quicker in the hot weather, and it was forecast to be a scorching summer. So first time they tried it (tried it? drank half a barrel, more like). In historical truth, it's hard to say which came first – drinking a half-barrel of scrumpy 40% proof cider, or hearing a snake warning them off the fruits of the tree of knowledge. 'It just wanted to keep us ignorant,' Adam said.

'Too late, man,' said Eve, 'come here, Big Boy.'

2 And as for Noah, I ask you… Heard this voice saying it's going to pee it down for months on end and drown the whole world. He looks round the total desert that stretches from one horizon to the opposite skyline, and says, rhetorically, 'Yeah? And where are you gonna get all the water from?'

Turning to Mrs Noah, he scoffed, 'Is it heck as going to rain – there's not a cloud in the sky. Get back to the planting, Naamah – we need the corn in the ground within the week.'

Boy! Did he build that ark fast!

3 You've heard of Abram? Or Abraham as he called himself later – not much of a disguise, that, was it? God sussed him out, just the same – and just to make sure he was paying attention and going to follow orders, he told Abraham to kill his only son.

'Hey?' Says Aby-Baby, 'This is the kind and benevolent Big Guy, is it?' But he don't get no answer, so he has a word with Isaac, his son, 'Look, Ize, he says, 'God thinks you're my son. How simple is he? Here's me, a hundred and fifteen years old – and you're fifteen, aren't you? Boaz was hanging round a lot back then, as I recall.'

187

Ize is wondering about where this is leading, but Abram's carrying on regardless, 'And he thinks you're mine. It's not as if the juniper and tamarind work as well as they're supposed to on the pothecary's adverts. So, Ize, we'll just tell him I killed you, and we'll change your name, like I did with mine, and you can grow a beard – he'll never cotton on.'

4 Moses? A double whammy, he was; deaf as a hitching post. 'A party in the Red Sea? Zippy? You hear it? Is that what that voice said?'

'Huh?' Zipporah, his equally deaf missus, said.

'There! Hear it? You need a party to help you to get away from the Egyptians.' So down he goes to the Red Sea with all this booze and trays heaped up with Ful Medames – the complete blend of mashed fava beans; kushari, a mixture of lentils, rice, pasta; molokhiya, chopped and cooked bush okra with garlic and coriander sauce; and feeter meshaltet. You know the kind of do – the full Google Menu.

Of course, Pharaoh hears about it, and gets in a bit of a huff. 'They can't have a party without inviting me,' he tells his army, 'We'll crash it.' So he turns up with all the chariots, and they all get stuffed and sloshed so bad they all pass out.

But the Israelites... Hebrews, they were then... wake up first because they're used to the heavy drinking side of life. 'Ay up,' they said. 'Big chance here. Let's do a runner while the tide's out.'

Course, when Pharaoh wakes up – still half-kaylied – him and his army go chasing after the slave gang, and don't even check the tide tables... Exit Pharaoh & Co.

5 And the other thing with Mosey-baby? 'I'm just going up Mount Sinai,' he tells them, 'to have a chat with the Big Guy. I'll see if he's got any rules to spare. If he charges for them, we'll have three. If they're free, we'll have a dozen, OK?'

Back he comes, forty days later, 'Sorry, lads. I was getting them all down, got to nine, and my chisel broke. And I says to myself, 'I can remember the next one, but the two after that... no... out my head completely. Big Guy isn't round any longer to remind me. So I'll just jot this last one down and we'll have to make do with ten, eh? How's that sound? Anybody got a spare chisel, while I still remember... er... Thou... shalt... not...' he chiselled away...

'Hang on, they're all a bit negative, aren't they?' Benyamin and Menasheh weren't going overboard for this.

Mosey paused and read them again. 'You're right, they are a bit. Ah well... Too late to change'em now.'

'It'll never catch on.'

6 David – he was another one. No, not *King* David – he never made it as King. No, he was just such a bloody nuisance they all called him fucking David. Or just 'kin David, so he didn't cotton on, and it sort of stuck. Anyway, there was this time when he's been on the ale all morning and he's a right prat, and gets all his smart gear on, silk slippers – they don't call them "slippers" for nothing. And him being well-oiled – not a good combination – slippers and oiled. Extra-long cloak on, feet tangled up in it. Everything was against him, and he went toppling down the stairs, all twenty-seven of them – supposed to be a lucky number. Broke his neck, laid out flat.

189

So the elders had a quick conflab, 'We need a replacement, quick. No not his sister – Abigail's no use.'

'Nor his wife – also Abigail. We'd never remember which was which. It's bad enough the way he's been carrying on with both of them.'

'Let's go for the other sister as David's substitute. Zeruiah's about the same size as him.' They had a very quick think about it, and decided, well before the Haggibborim arrived.

Yeah, right pack of Heroes, they were. 'Get his royal raiment off, quick. Plenty of make-up on Zeruiah. Maybe some black dotty bits to look like a beard. Nobody will ever know. Come on, then, chop chop – lots to do before the banquet.'

7   Not to mention Samson. Sure, he does all the killing with the ass's jawbone thing, but then he goes shouting his mouth off to Queen Delilah. Silly lummox told her, 'My strength comes because I don't cut my hair.' I tried that. It doesn't work. My wife said I'd better get to the barber smartish, or she'd clout me. She did, too.

So, you know the story: Delilah gets him drunk, and the Big Guy can't take his ale. Bad as David, he is. And she cut his hair. He wakes up weak as a tadpole in May, and she promptly blinds him, just out of spite.

'I happened to have a couple of hot irons handy,' she shruggs. 'Besides, he was crap in bed – stiff as a jaffa jelly.

So she stays safe as Queen of the Philistines, and, a year later, she decides to have an anniversary party.

'Yes, Majesty, but what's the Star Attraction?' The courtiers asked, rather pointedly.

'Brill idea,' she says, and hauls Samson out of his dungeon to be the main feature at the party. But, one look at him, 'He's all filthy and gruesome, shaggy-haired. He's not coming to my party like that. Get the barbers in, and the cleaners. Spruce him up.'

So there he is, all sparkling and not too happy at the party. He heaves and tugs on the pillars, and of course, nothing happens – a right laugh, he was. Everybody agreed, and cheered and chucked beer at him before he was carted back down to his cellar, really chalked off.

But – and it's a big, Samson-saving, but – the party just went on and on, because Deiliah was so chuffed at still being Queen, when it's Wham! Bam! Thankyou Big Guy – and there's an earthquake. The whole palace went tumbling down like David down the steps. And, naturally, Samson, squashed and buried under all the rubble back in his dungeon, was given the credit.

Then we come to Jesus. Even before he was born, things didn't work out too well for him and his martyr complex. Like when they went to Bethlehem that Christmas. They arrived just after sunset at a three-star inn, Joseph and Mary the Virgin – that was what they called her at the Dog and Garter, anyway. Sort of sarcastic joke. You know, *Mary the Virgin*, nudge, nudge. They go up to the girl in Reception, 'You are so in luck,' she says, 'we've just had a cancellation: the Honeymoon Suite's free. The people who had the booking had some bother on the road to Damascus, and they can't get. It's okay; you can have it for the same price as the stable stalls.'

'We'll take it,' says Mary, whose back was playing her up.

'But it won't help our image,' pipes up Joseph, 'lodging in the poshest room in the place. Would you mind, if anyone asks, saying that we had to bed down with the donkeys? It'll look better on our CV.'

9 Then there was that time when Jesus turned up at the temple. A right bee in his bonnet, he had, going on about all the robber merchants and sellers of religious fakes and lending money, exchanging it for Roman coin and all that sort of thing. 'What are you on about, you great Jessie? This is the market. What are we supposed to do in the market?'

'No,' he says, 'it's the temple.'

'Is it chuff?' they come back at him. 'There's a line of bricks over there, set into the ground to mark the boundary. Didn't you see them?'

That Jesus lad was not too bright. That little incident got him marked down as a trouble-maker on his school report, it did.

10 And that nearly went against him later, when he was up on charges of stirring things up in Jerusalem. He wasn't well-travelled, you know – Bethlehem is only half an hour south of Jerusalem these days; maybe half a day back then. The Romans had the right idea, 'They're obviously trumped-up charges,' Pontius Pilate tells the crowd. 'Jesus was saying people should obey the law and pay their taxes. Obviously not guilty.'

But the Jews were squabbling among themselves again and kept going on about it.

So Pontius Pilate joined up with Herod Antipas and got him off the hook. 'I'm not here to cater to a load of irritated Israelites; he's just a martyr wannabe.'

'Yeah, he never did any harm, apart from that time at the temple. But that's only his juvenile record, so it can't be entered as evidence.'

'Suppose we crucify the thieving, riotous maniac they keep calling Bar Abbas – which just means Son of the Father, generally used as a John Doe sort of name – like Fred Bloggs.'

'So? What? We crucify him, keep the crowd well back and nobody'll be able to tell who it is, anyway?'

'Sounds like a winner to me.'

'Please, please. Tell everybody it was me,' Jesus kept telling them, 'I really need the publicity for this new religion I'm starting.'

Finishing his brief talk, Merda Agitatore checked behind him, a swift glance – the emergency exit was right there, partly open, as per his stipulation.

'Now then,' he re-addressed his audience, 'Any questions?'

THE OLD ENGLISH ARMS

'There's this thing on Facebook, Coll.'

'Of course there is. There's always something on Face-Effing-Book. What isn't?' Not my scheme at all, Facebook. I don't do *Social*.

I glance now and again because my twin bullies, er, sisters insist. 'You need to keep abreast of the social world. Look – there's this group from when you were at Art College. They're all meeting up again.' Alice had this penetrating look that meant she was up to something.

'That's fifteen years ago,' I said. 'Why would I want to?'

But Jenny, especially, kept on about it. There was only a year between me and sibs, so we pretty much went round with the same crowd at the time; we knew the same people, but, looking at the on-screen photo, I could only think of half a dozen names, and as many faces. 'I haven't a clue which names match which faces. Come on, Jen, I was busy with my art then. Remember? I was the worker? The one who was *so* keen.' Yeah, okay, so it didn't get me far, but I tried. I really believed in myself. Huh.

Then Jenny's got me by the throat and her teeth are locked together. 'You *shall* go, Coll. Arrabella will child-mind.'

Alice agreed, with menaces.

So it's both of you, a conspiracy. Or frontal attack, as I prefer to think of it. 'Go where?'

'To The Old English Arms in Wintercotes, with an Indian at the Curry Parlour afterwards. Tomorrow night. There's thirteen already who've said they'll go. And we said we would, as well.'

'Including you.'

'Where's all this come from?' My suspicion was deep, deep, deep.

'You've been invited. Specifically. By name. On Facebook. *See?'*

'Who's that?' I peered at the inviter's face. 'Never seen her before. Her name's what? Callista? New to me.'

'She mentioned you by name.' Alice had that extra-devious look about her.

'Along with a dozen others.'

'No, it's just you she invited.'

'Why would I want to see somebody I never saw before?'

'It's all fixed. You're coming.'

There's no fighting Jenny and Alice when they're in a monthly mood. 'Yes, I remember some,' I admitted, looking round the spread-out cluster in the Old English's lounge bar. Jacks and Delia were there – Married; I see them round town occasionally. Five kids. Fat bloke called Eric, as I remember… and the short girl with black hair… Sue something? Most faces looked vaguely familiar. 'There's nobody I remember vividly, Jen. Girls or fellers. Sorry. Can I go now? Arrabella will—'

'No, you can't! You'll have a glass of Italian Spritz and like it. And you'll join in or I'll make you watch Emmerdale for a week.' Jenny can be ruthlessly vicious like that.

'You know I can't— *don't* drink.'

'Sit down, Colin.' She gave me the last-warning dire threat look and pushed me onto a red-embroidered seat – same as they have at the Curry Parlour. 'That's her, talking with Alice near the bar.'

Thin face, blonde. 'Never seen her before. I want to go home.' I racked my brain – what's left of it. Did she look at all familiar? 'Possibly, if I do a brain-strain… maybe yes. She looks vaguely familiar. That name's not right, though?'

Alice was pointing at me. The girl… woman looked at me, deadpan, and came over, 'I'm glad you came, Colin.'

She plonked herself in front of me.

Seems vaguely familiar. Maybe… 'Er, sorry, remind me, your name?' *God, this is so awkward.*

'I'm Callista.' She looked at me like it should mean something.

'You… you… remind me of… someone.'

'Jilly?' she prompted. Looking hopeful that it would prompt a memory.

That was it, yes… It was seeping in. 'Erm, I'm terrible at remembering. Jilly, yes. Jilly…'

'It's what you always called me – after that painting we did of the Queen of the Dance. You remember?'

It was coming back, so slowly. 'Yes… yes. It became like I thought Jilly was really your name.' Bright, super face. Yes, I did remember; she was a laugh. Back then. *Younger then, too. How stupid can I think? Not someone I was close with, though? Not much overlap; more like I was on one side of the gang and she on the other.*

She was chattering on. I knew not what about. Yes, the balanced desk trick was me. You, too? And fetching that cat out the manhole pit.

197

'Oh, was it you I passed it to? I forget. And at the bowling?'

'Yes! We were partners when we won the Wintercotes cup...' She was so sparkly bright-eyed.

'It's coming back to me, yes.' I felt quite warm to her then. And other things were coming back... 'We had some nights out? Nights in... Down the match... Rambles round Derbyshire... Yes...? That was us?'

It hurt to remember, to think back. 'I don't recollect things too well, sometimes. Sorry.'

'I've been in Australia since, Colin. In Adelaide. You don't recall? How's our little girl? What did you call her?'

Damn... what is she on about? Our girl? Daughter? *Ours?* What is she saying?

'She is still alive, isn't she?' *You don't need to look so doubting.*

Hellfire. Flooding back. So buried. I couldn't... I was getting up. Jenny was behind me. I felt her hands on my shoulders, 'Down boy.'

She – Jilly – reached and took my hand, smiling. All stupidly sympathetic-like. As if I need that.

Jenny's hands pressed again, nosy moo listening in. I wasn't having that. Not letting her pry into anything that happened. *What did happen? It's* Jenny who knows already. She remembers a lot more than I do. She tells me bits. Always saying odd little things, like to remind me. *Invent me, more like.*

'My daughter? She's not—' I was going to say "ours" but... but it was coming back... yes, she was... *is.* 'Er, she's okay,' I'm saying, on automatic. 'Arrabella, I called her.'

'*Okay!?!?!?!*' Jenny comes exploding into my right ear. 'You have the world's most beautiful fourteen-year-old daughter and you say *"she's okay"?* What sort of moron—? No... Coll... No... sorry. I didn't mean that.'

Calling me a moron... I'm not. I'm not. But it's not meant badly; she just says it when she's impatient with me. She means well. It's because I'm slow to get words together sometimes; don't come bursting out with love and life all the time. The way Jenny bursts out with love and life, I'm amazed she hasn't had twenty babies by now.

I'm still me inside. Me? Yeah, sure. My brain's still wrapped round a bullet, but I'm still me.

Sisters can be cruel sometimes, can't they?

'My kids love me,' I'm saying, in my standard mantra. 'They understand me.'

'Kids? Plural?' This Jilly was eager, rubbing the back of my hand. It didn't encourage or reassure me. *Oh shuggs. What have Jenny and Alice lined me up for?*

'Yes, yes, yes. Arrabella... is your daughter – *our* daughter. She's the pseudo-mum for the littlies.

'You're married, then?'

I was all froze up then. *You must know. I can't tell you about Mendolita. But you're looking at me. Waiting.* She kept hold of my hand. It felt scary. Long time. Jenny was like half whispering, behind me. *And mouthing, I bet.*

'I... I married Mendolita. Was she at college? You remember her? No? Tall. Gentle. Calm face? Two years below us. I'm rambling, aren't I? The kids are lucky; they took after her, not me.'

'There was... something happened,' Alice had me cornered, as well. 'Tell her, Coll.'

Trapped. Three of them, Pinned me down. In the lounge bar. No escape. 'Mendolita was... hurt... she died. And I died, too.'

I stumbled it out, but Jenny had told her already, I could tell. Christmas four years ago. Some terrorist opened fire round the shops in Nottingham. They shot him, too. They got me back alive, at the hospital. I didn't want to, not without Mendolita. Except I had four little kids to look after. I think that was why they bothered with me – only because of the Fab Four.

I'm the same as I was before. I think the same things. I just don't talk so much, not out the house, anyway. Not as much as Jenny. Or the kids.

Jenny was coming out from behind me – that triumphant gloating look she gets. And she sat with *her*. And was telling her things. *I wish you wouldn't. Not all at once. It'd be for me to tell her – and I don't want to.* Things that sank. Long time ago. All things gone and sucked down and covered over.

My own sister digging them back up, like going round with a great big spade. Things about me. And my kids. And the single picture I had... Of you, Callista. I framed it specially for Arrabella, 'She's your mum,' I tell her. I think she keeps it in a drawer she hardly ever goes near.

Jenny's telling her about my work at home. *Why's she telling her this?* Making me out to be some sort of Capability Brown meets the Angel of the North – just because I design and create gardens and sculptures for *very* rich people. Course, the kids go with me on our consultations and workings – huge motorhome like film stars have. Maybe not that grand, but we're doing okay. The kids love the freedom.

What have you come back for? You left. Went to Australia. Fourteen years ago.

She's coming round tomorrow. To meet my children. Especially Arrabella, of course. I told Arrabella she was coming. She already knows things about her mum. I always told her that her mum loved her: it was *her* parents who did their nuts and couldn't cope with her having a baby. 'They tried to make her have an abortion, but it was too late, and she had you – such a tiny little girl, you were. But they suddenly emigrated, not a word to anyone – total secret. And made her go to Oz with them and would have left you here to be adopted.'

'But you wanted me, eh, Dad?'

'Mmm, I couldn't have somebody else adopting *my* child.'

Jenny's really scared in case I turn weird. It's why she hovers behind me so much. 'I don't need you hanging round my neck tomorrow, Jenny. So stay away. Nothing for you to worry about; Callista will be scared, too. But I won't turn funny or do anything.'

I'm thinking it's super that Arrabella's mum's come back, even if it's just to see her for a time.

Or just maybe really get to know her.

We always liked each other's art stuff.

I think I'd really like her to stay longer, now I remember so much.

SOLOMON GRUNDY

My girlfriend – little treasure that she is – threw me out the house on Monday, because *she* was playing round and needed elbow room. 'Leg room, more like,' I suggested as I finished picking up my clothes from the pavement and collecting a smack across the face for daring to voice an opinion that didn't involve her and "wonderful".

I slept at a hostel that night and went into work on Tuesday – I'm a courier driver and escort for RushJobz
'Two packages out the front store have gone missing overnight,' Despatcher Dave tells me, 'So what do you know about that? Where were you last night?'
'The hostel on Gleeton Street.'
'Sarky bastard,' He gave me the really-irritated look. So I got sacked on Tuesday.

George at the hostel told me about a one-off delivery job he was doing on Wednesday – driving 120 miles each way. He needed an escort and/or driver.
So, Wednesday dinner, after a long drive up the M1, we were knocking at the door of this massive mansion-type house near Leeds. Half-way through the second round of knocking, pushing dead door bells, banging on the window and shouting, the whole place fell in on us – massive police raid. All rampaging, bellowing and smashing doors and people down. I got coshed with one of them huge door-breaker things, and trampled on by a thousand boots.

Next thing I know, I'm under arrest for some sort of contraband smuggling. They didn't say what, and I was in no fit state to ask – going black, blue and yellow with nasty red patches all over. Jaw felt a bit, er, locked-up, too. Couldn't speak, so they put me down as uncooperative. I mean, you courier something and you always ask for full details of what it is – Yeah, right. Brown cardboard pack Two by Two and bloody heavy, is the most you even think about, and you never, ever, wonder. I never even saw the parcel till I pulled it out the back of the van in Leeds.

I didn't get any better in a cell overnight. Managed a drink of extra-watery orange, but they didn't have straws for me to eat the crusty egg and charred sausage with, so they had to take me to A&E on Thursday. I wasn't well enough to scream and moan, so nobody bothered much with me. And the fuzz were apparently happy enough to sit about, drinking tea and chatting up the nurses for six hours. Then the new shift got round to it, and brought a doctor to see me. They admitted me when they saw all the discolouring round my ribs and stomach. Started muttering… 'Internal hemmer-something… Septi-seemy-thingy.'

I dunno, I was out of it by then. They did something medical to me, and kept me in "Observation" overnight with two fuzz sitting round reading newspapers.

It was docs' rounds on Friday. They pulled faces and carted me off, talking about drains and anti-biotics and full blood change… and brain damage. I didn't get much of that. I think I was out cold, though I remember bits in an operating theatre. Aren't they bright in there? The lights, not so much the confused-seeming docs.

They didn't seem too happy with me when I came round. They wheeled me into I See You, where they monitored me all day and all night, every hour. The fuzz had vanished. Like a miracle, that was. Didn't miss them.

Come Saturday morning – late, because it was the weekend – a pair of little student docs came to see me, looking at my charts and things like they were Chinese. The docs were Chinese, too, so that was okay. Head-shaking and mumbling appeared to be the order of the day. Then they saw my name – and kept repeating it… 'Sororom Glundy.' I kid you not – they actually said it like that. And started reciting the rhyme… 'Sororom Glundy, born on Mundy…'

And they got to Friday – 'Got worse on Flyday.' They nodded to each other, like it was a successful diagnosis, summary and prediction rolled into one.

'Saturday?' They kept trying to remember Saturday… 'Saturday? What happen Saturday?'

'Died on Saturday,' I helped them out.

'Ah yes! Die on Saturday.'

'Okay, so now you know.'

And off they went, happy to have conveyed the prognosis to me.

I checked the wall clock – midday.

I've got twelve hours left, max.

A BEAUTIFUL PAIR

Browsing round the shop, I didn't need any assistance; I knew what I was looking for and didn't want to be pestered. Everything I wanted was on the shelves, and I often went there so I knew my way round the whole place, where to look for what I wanted. A nod and a smile to the staff was enough for us all.

Two of the young servers were behind the counter; Jerry was laughing with his big-nosed colleague – I think they call him Beaky Pete, 'Here, look, I'm getting some more pics through to my mobile.'

They started looking through them, turning the screen this way and that, laughing and gasping in amazement... disbelief... wonder. ''Wow, look at that pair.' Peering closer, expanding the picture.

'Best I've ever seen.'

'Whoa... See the tits there?'

Beaky Pete had his own phone out by then, and they started comparing pictures and videos, 'Oh, just look at this pair...' Laughing and whooping, glancing round the shop, eyes glinting, 'I'll send you that one...'

'Hey, let's have one of her. Jeez, look at them'

'I never seen tits like'em.'

A couple of other customers had come in by then, a man and a pink-clad woman with her nose in the air. They were looking at some of the goods on the shelves near the counter, muttering as they compared prices and sizes. Obviously listening in, they kept glancing and staring at the admiring, phone-wrapped twosome.

Mr Gaffey, the boss, came through from the back, looking round, 'Anyone waiting to be served? No? Are you alright, sir, madam? Need any help?' Pinkie and partner sniffed negatively.

He exchanged a nod and a mutual-recognition smile with me, and joined his two employees behind the counter, beginning to check the till roll until he noticed their conversation. After glancing round again, he joined in, mobile out, and delightedly displaying his own collection of photos and video clips, 'I got these last week... Look at this pair here.'

They were in raptures; laughing, gloating over the images they each cherished, glancing round... I was still looking and making my mind up about whether to buy the small one, or go for the larger model – checking the specs again. And ear-wigging, of course.

The middle-aged couple were distinctly ruffled. The lady in pink suddenly turned round, looking ready to explode, mouth opening wide in affronted rage, 'How dare you,' she started, 'what filthy minds you have.'

Just as the three staff burst out in renewed delight at the latest image to come up, 'Oh Wow... this pair of tits!'

'The plumage on that one.'

'What a pair they make.'

'See the flight feathers on the long-tail tit?'

'And that pair of bullfinches.'

'We're getting them in stock?'

'Yep - next week, now we've got the GL18 licence for British wild birds.'

'A nice addition to parrots and budgies, eh?'

'Yes, madam, sorry,' the boss looked up, beaming, 'Are you interested in finches and tits? We have a special introductory offer for next week.'

Even my Australian King Parrot has never shivered her wings and ruffled her feathers as swiftly as our enraged

Pink Lady somehow managed that day. Out she stalked, muttering in exactly the same way my Yellow-crested Booby does when she doesn't get her wicked way with the cuttlefish bone.

ABOUT THE AUTHOR

Trevor is a Nottinghamshire, UK writer. His short stories and poems have frequently won prizes, and he has appeared on television discussing local matters.

As well as SF short stories, he has published many reader-friendly books and articles, mostly about volcanoes around the world, and dinosaur footprints on Yorkshire's Jurassic coast.

He spent fourteen years at the classroom chalkface; sixteen as headteacher of a special school; and sixteen as an Ofsted school inspector to round it off. His teacher wife now jokes that it's "Sleeping with the Enemy".

In the 1980s, his Ph.D. research pioneered the use of computers in the education of children with profound learning difficulties.

BY THE SAME AUTHOR

OF OTHER TIMES AND SPACES

The Giant Anthology – 460 pages with 39 tales of here and now, and the futures that await us.

If you were spying on another planet, would you do any better than Dicky and Miriam in the snappy two-pager "Air Sacs and Frilly Bits".

Could you live among the laughs and lovers of "I'm a Squumaid"? Or cope with the heartache of "The Twelve Days of Crystal-Ammas"?

In the novella-length "The Colonist", how could anyone fault Davvy's actions in setting up Hill Six-Four-Six with a party of Highraff refugee women and children?

How might you cope in class with the all-knowing "Thank you, Mellissa" and her little yellow ducks? Would you be the guide for Reju Royalty when they insist on "Watching the Scurrugs"? Are we truly destined for the same fate that awaits this universe in "A Little Co-operation"?

AMAZON READER REVIEWS

–   "Sci-fi at its most original"
–   "Absolutely excellent, equal with anything I have read in the genre, including all the old masters when I was a kid."
–   "Great entertainment and good stories from start to finish."
     – "A sci-fi feast – I highly recommend it."

The New-Classic Sci-Fi Series

Details of contents of all books are on Trevor's website at www.sci-fi-author.com. Exact details of timing for the release of later books will find their way there as soon as they are known. Hopeful speculation about the target dates litters the blog you can find there.

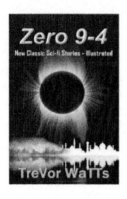

Book 1 in the New-Classic Series of Sci-Fi from the Lighter Side.
AMAZON READER REVIEWS
"Loved the sheer variety on offer"
"A great book of short stories to delight any sci-fi reader's palette"
"Go on, give yourself treat!"

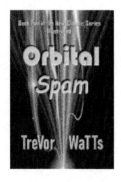

Book 2 in the New-Classic Series of Sci-Fi from the Lighter Side.
AMAZON READER REVIEWS
"A great selection"
"A heads up on this third one I've read by this author"
"My kind of real characters – I get their humour and dilemmas and problems and solutions – or failures, sometimes."

Book 3 in the New-Classic Series.
READER REVIEWS

"5* because it's basically the best sci-fi I've read for years."

"Surprised I was so taken up with these stories – Excellent."

"Completely absorbed in some of these situations – the atmosphere and the so-believable characters."

BOOKS TO COME

Book 4 in the New-Classic Series.
READER REVIEWS

So you have an affair with a Tangerine, but did you expect this to happen?

Morris was desperate for Fame, but this?

Can Mz Dainty possibly pass her space-pilot driving test in the midst of so much chaos?

In the next three minutes, can you call the right shot when the enemy's High Space Drifter comes barrelling towards you?

Book 5 in the New-Classic Sci-Fi Series.

Under interrogation, would you give them the secret of Vondur'Eye, regardless of the consequences?

What comes shimmering along the beach?

Effo the maths genius has forgotten… what?

Your colony ship's suffered a breach – Level 1. So where does your future lie now?

Roads Less Travelled

The second collection in the odds, sods & surprises series of short stories from the Silver Side. (OsssOssss2).

You think *you've* had problems with your satnav?

What's on the menu tonight at the Truckers' Brass Kettle Diner?

Igor, the traffic warden, will not be moved..

Is there something promising, or threatening, about the woman in the car in the other lane?

Worlds of Wonder
Book of Poetry

Collected poems that everyone
Can see themselves reflected in.
Of flower-strewn girls, of ponies gone,
A ranch-hand wreaks the deadly sin.

Filling up the parting glass;
Of cats and men and ladies, too.
World War One and graves en masse;
Of dynamite and the Devil's brew.

Machu Picchu and Galway Town
Whoever said Old men don't fall?
From Java's mud to nature's gown
The pages here unveil them all

Minimum arrestable delinquency;
The haggis that truly took my heart;
In elegant idiosyncrasy
I take my leave, I must depart.

Taking it Personally
OsssOssss3

Thirty-five short stories about the
things that people do.
What The Boss said was most
regrettable, but he has to live with
it.
Would Uncle Dave allow the thieving
creature into his cardboard castle?
You think you're in the cells for a
night? Think again.

216

A FEW NOTES

 A category 4 name – that truly was the sequence of tropical storms that year. And the Cat Rescue named their new strays in that way.

Retail Fever (with thanks to John Masefield's Sea fever) was written in the early weeks of the first Covid19 lockdown 2020, and I really missed Morissons.

Vechi Sânge's Coughing Fit was inspired by the green man on the noticeboard while I waited for a blood test in the doctor's waiting room in Eastwood.

Year 9 was inspired by many very frazzled teachers I met when I was a school inspector – they had my 100% sympathy for their plight.

Bisoprolol very much reflects my experiences with this medication, and others.

Baksheesh Bill was my step-father, RIP.

A Bolt from the Blue is closely based on my experiences in Players Cigarette Factory, Nottingham when I was a student in the sixties.

I was sitting in a Notcutts garden centre café, and a nun did give me a huge beaming smile, as though she knew me. It was unnerving. That was a lull between lockdowns.

Three Silver Buttons – I had this brief encounter on Chesterfield Market, and extended it in the café ten minutes later.

"Dwindling" was the title for a poetry competition commemorating centennial of the WW 1 armistice. It won.

Doctor Johnson – I rarely insist on my title, just when someone is being deliberately discourteous.

Stefff – is me. My brothers really are 'two halves' like that. But there the similarities end. We get on fine.

The Ten Command Moments was an hour of mischief.

A Beautiful Pair was inspired by a similar, innocent incident in a tropical fish shop I frequent. Fish, not finches at Wharf Aquatics.

These stories all have their own back-story. I feel very attached to most of them – if not all of them.

 I use images I've either drawn from scratch, or assembled and adapted from internet images. Vector-Stock and Dreamstime are good places to buy them, among others. But there are millions of free-pics out there. I use a combination of Paint, ACDSee and Xara to play with them.

To mention a few: The waitress pic in The Prim Reaper is from freepik @ vectorstock.com

Pics of hospital beds, the Busker, and the Settled kind of guy are from iconfinder

The parachuting cat icon is based on action-2483689_1280 from Pin-clipart.

 TrevorW

Printed in Great Britain
by Amazon

65058057R00129